MONARCH
OF THE SANDS

MONARCH OF THE SANDS

BY

SHARON KENDRICK

First published in Great Britain 2011
by Mills & Boon, an imprint of Harlequin (UK) Limited.
Large Print edition 2012
Harlequin (UK) Limited, Eton House,
18-24 Paradise Road, Richmond, Surrey TW9 1SR

© Sharon Kendrick 2011

ISBN: 978 0 263 22543 3

Harlequin (UK) policy is to use papers that are natural,
renewable and recyclable products and made from
wood grown in sustainable forests. The logging and
manufacturing process conform to the legal environmental
regulations of the country of origin.

Printed and bound in Great Britain
by CPI Antony Rowe, Chippenham, Wiltshire

With special thanks to Dr Lloyd Wood—
whose passion about oil discovery
was contagious and helped
make my heroine's father become real.

And to Sarah of Smart Bitches,
who inadvertently inspired this story.

CHAPTER ONE

AGAINST her pale skin, the diamond flashed like a shooting star and Frankie gazed at it in wonder. Who would ever have thought it? Geeky, freaky Frankie O'Hara engaged to be married—and sporting a solitaire the size of a blueberry.

Spreading out her fingers, she watched as the precious stone caught the pale November light and glittered it back at her. Her father would have smiled and said that a diamond was nothing but a hard and highly refractive form of carbon—but to Frankie it was so much more than that. It was a symbol. It signified that a man loved her and wanted to spend the rest of his life with her. A handsome, successful man, too. Not the kind of man she'd ever have thought would be attracted to someone like her—not in the million or so years it took to make a diamond.

The low roar of a car disturbed her dreamy thoughts and Frankie blinked with surprise and a slight feeling of panic. Surely Simon wasn't here already? Why, she hadn't peeled a single potato for the celebration meal she'd been planning—and surely the chicken breasts hadn't been marinating for nearly long enough?

She peered out of the window and the breath caught sharply in her throat as she saw the expensive and gleaming vehicle which was making its way up the drive, spraying little shoals of gravel in its wake.

That certainly wasn't Simon—who drove a comfortable saloon indistinguishable from the many others which dominated the roads of this affluent area of suburban England. The car which was now pulling to a halt in front of the house was sporty, black and powerful and looked as if it would be more at home on an international racing circuit than in this quiet corner of the world. And she didn't have to look at the driver's hard profile to know exactly who was driving it.

Zahid!

Her heart began to pound and Frankie's mouth became parchment-dry. After all, the man in question was pretty close to every woman's fantasy man and he was sitting right outside her house. Zahid Al Hakam—royal Sheikh and King. The man with the hard, hawklike features and the dark, enigmatic eyes.

It was highly unusual for someone as ordinary as Frankie to be friends with an exotic and powerful sheikh, but life often had funny twists and turns along the way. The sheikh's father had been a long-time friend of her father's, so she'd known the Prince of Khayarzah ever since she'd been a little girl—though his visits had tapered away since he had unexpectedly become King. The sudden death of his uncle and his cousin had left Zahid as the heir apparent—with no time in his busy diary to visit old friends in small English towns.

At first, she'd missed his visits dreadfully, before deciding that his absence was probably all for the best—because hadn't she wasted too many hours fantasising about a man who was way out of her league?

She glanced out of the window again. So why had he just turned up out of the blue? And why today, of all days?

She saw him get out of the car—unfolding his long-legged frame with the lithe elegance which always made her think of a jungle cat. He slammed the car door but didn't bother locking it—though, come to think of it, he'd probably stationed his security people at the end of the drive. And besides, who would dare try and steal *his* car?

The pealing of the doorbell galvanised her into life—and as she rushed to answer it she thought that wasn't the only thing which was peeling. The walls badly needed painting. The big house was inevitably showing signs of wear and tear—despite her best efforts to try to maintain the place. And didn't that only reinforce Simon's increasingly urgent suggestion that she sell the family home and the valuable land on which it stood?

Heart still pounding, she pulled open the door and psyched herself up to greet him, praying that she might have grown up and moved on enough not to be affected by him. Five long years had passed since she'd last seen him—surely enough time to give her some kind of immunity against him.

Vain hope. She swallowed, trying to quell the rush of guilty longing which made her heart begin to race as she stared into his stern face. Because was there a woman on earth who could have been unmoved by his presence—even if they had just agreed to marry someone else?

He wasn't how most people expected a sheikh to look—with not a flowing robe in sight—but that was deliberate. Years ago, he had told her that he liked to blend in—like the chameleon who adapted its appearance to its habitat in order to survive. That was the reason why he was fluent in several languages and spoke them like a native. Except that someone as rugged and as powerful as Zahid could never really *blend* in. No matter what he said or wore, he drew the eye and caught people's attention, just as a beautiful bloom tossed on a dusty roadside might have done.

Clad in a beautifully cut grey suit, which showcased the musculature of his magnificent body, he completely dominated the doorway of her house. Eyes like chips of black stone surveyed her from a hawk-featured face, his skin a shade lighter than burnished copper. With that raven-dark hair, he looked like some brooding movie-star of yesteryear, she thought, with a sudden and unwanted ache. He was all stillness and silence—while managing to exude a raw and undeniable animal magnetism.

For some inexplicable reason, Frankie plunged her left hand deep into the pocket of her jeans and a wave of guilt shivered through her. Was she *trying to hide her brand-new engagement ring?* And *why on earth was she doing that?*

'Hello, Zahid,' she said.

Few people—and especially commoners—were permitted to use his first name, but Zahid wasn't thinking about protocol at that moment.

For a moment there was complete silence as his gaze raked over her in astonishment. Surely there must be some kind of mistake?

'Francesca?' His eyes narrowed—as if he'd been confronted by a mirage in the middle of the desert. 'Is that really you?'

Frankie tried not to react. *Nobody* called her Francesca. Nobody except him. She heard the familiar way he curled the syllables around his tongue and a stupid little shiver whispered over her skin. It was a name given to her by her glamorous mother who had been hoping for a mini-me and been bitterly disappointed. When the duckling child had stubbornly refused to become a swan, the exotic tag had disappeared and been replaced by the much more workaday 'Frankie' and that was what she'd been ever since. But not to Zahid.

'Of course it's me!' she said, but she wouldn't have been human if she hadn't felt a sudden rush of pleasure at that flash of very grown-up appreciation in his eyes. He'd never looked at her in any way other than the way he might have re-

garded a faithful retainer. A loyal servant, say—
or a pet dog who came running over with its tail
wagging eagerly. She knew that her question was
an unnecessary one but she wanted to hear how
Zahid would answer it. 'Why, do I look different?'

He felt a flicker of something unexpected.
Damned right she did. Different didn't even
come close to it. Last time he'd seen her, she'd
been a tomboyish nineteen-year-old, so nonde-
script and shapeless that you'd never have noticed
her in a crowd. So what the hell had happened
in the intervening years?

He studied her closely. The short hair, which
used to stick out at odd angles, had been allowed
to grow so that now it fell in dark, silken waves
down her back. The thick, geeky glasses had disappeared and instead he could see a pair of eyes
which were a deep shade of startling blue. And
the shapeless clothes she used to wear had been
replaced by a pair of snug jeans and a soft oat-
meal sweater, which hinted at a body he would
never have imagined Francesca possessing.

'What the hell happened to your glasses?' he demanded unevenly.

'Oh, I wear contacts now.' She shrugged. 'Everybody does.'

He wanted to ask when had she developed such an amazing pair of breasts and a bottom which was curvier than a scimitar? He wanted to know when the dramatic transformation from girl to woman had taken place—but he stopped himself by biting back the faintly erotic questions. Because this was *Francesca* he was talking to— sweet, innocent little Francesca—not some potential lover he'd just met at a cocktail party.

Instead, he fixed her with a cool look, which was intended to remind her that although he was a family friend of long-standing he still expected a degree of formality and protocol.

Frankie saw the faint furrow which had appeared on his brow and correctly interpreted it. 'Oh, forgive me! Would you...?' She opened the door a little wider, unable to decide whether she wanted him to go or to stay. Because if he stayed—wouldn't it unsettle her? Wouldn't it risk starting those stupid fantasies again—the ones she used to get whenever he strode into the house? The ones which had always ended with Zahid scooping her up in his arms and starting to kiss her before telling her that he couldn't live without her. 'Would you like to come in?' she finished weakly.

No, he'd driven down from London to stand on her doorstep like a salesman! 'Thanks,' he said drily, and walked into the hallway—a place which was at once both alien and familiar to him. A large and faintly shabby English home with a big, green garden. Yet hadn't this been the one place outside his homeland where he had always been able to kick back and relax? A place where nobody watched him or where there were no indiscreet gossips or the threat of someone talking to the press. Because being the sheikh's nephew meant that you were always watched; always listened to.

Over the years, his father used to bring him here—to talk to the man who had changed the course of his country's history. Francesca's brilliant and eccentric geologist father. It had been his unexpected discovery of oil which had lifted Khayarzah out of the crippling debts caused by decades of warfare—and changed its whole future.

As Francesca shut the door behind him Zahid found his gaze lingering for longer than usual on her unexpectedly blue eyes, remembering seeing her soon after she'd been born. What a mewling little creature she'd been—with her bright red face screaming out from amid a swathe of white blankets. He'd have been, what—thirteen at the time?

He remembered the way she used to waddle up to him as a chubby-faced toddler—unbelievably cute—and the way she'd demand to be carried by him just before she first started school. And hadn't he done as she'd asked? Allowed her to twist him round her little finger in a way which no woman had ever done before, nor since.

He remembered, too, the cold air of neglect and despair which settled on the house when her mother left, pronouncing herself bored with her older, scientist husband. She'd run off with someone richer. Someone who had shown her the finer things in life. The first of the many wealthy lovers who would ultimately dump her before she died in a car crash, a tragedy sullied by the shame of knowing that the car was being driven by a prominent and very married politician.

But Francesca and her father had rallied. They'd formed a tight little unit. The little girl had grown up surrounded by scientists and left largely to her own devices. Consequently, she hadn't gone through the coy teenage years—or the stage of showing off her body with minuscule clothes. In fact, up until this precise moment you would barely have noticed she was a woman at all.

He remembered teaching her how to play cards when she'd been unhappy at school. And actually letting her beat him! He was deeply and instinctively competitive, and it was the only time in his life that he hadn't insisted on winning. It had been worth it just to see the little smile which had briefly illuminated her troubled features.

A voice broke into his thoughts and he realised she was speaking to him. 'Did you say something?' he questioned, shaking his head a little because it was unlike him to be sentimental.

'I was asking what had brought you here, to Surrey.' She tipped her head to one side. 'Or were you just passing?'

For a moment he didn't answer. What *had* brought him here today? The realisation that he hadn't seen her in nearly five years and the faint guilt which had accompanied that thought? He knew that she was alone in the world now—and though he'd always intended to keep an eye on her, life just somehow kept getting in the way. And ever since the unexpected crown had been placed on his head just eighteen months ago the restrictions imposed by his new role had piled down thick and fast.

'I have business in London, so I thought I'd do a detour,' he said. 'To see how you are. Realising that it is quite some time since I last saw you— and that I really ought to do something about it.'

He was looking at her in such an odd and piercing way that Frankie could feel colour stealing into her cheeks.

'Would you…would you like a drink?' she asked, knowing that he rarely accepted any kind of sustenance. She used to wonder if it was because he always had to be careful about someone trying to poison him until her father explained that royals always liked to keep a certain amount of distance about them, no matter where they were.

'Yes, I would.'

'You would?'

He knitted his eyebrows together. 'Didn't you just offer me a drink—or have I started hearing things? And if you offer something, then it's usually expected you'll provide it. Tea, please. Mint—if you have it.'

Nervously, she nodded, wishing that he'd disappear for a moment, leaving her to compose herself. So she could slip her engagement ring off until after he'd gone—thus postponing the inevitable questions she had no desire to answer even though she wasn't quite sure why that was. 'Would you…would you like to wait in the sitting room?'

Zahid frowned. What the hell was the matter with her today? He began to wonder if her dramatic physical transformation was responsible for her odd and rather secretive attitude? 'No. I'll come into the kitchen and talk to you while you're making it—that's what I usually do.'

'Yes.' But usually she didn't feel this odd and prickling kind of awareness fizzing in the air around them. As if something had changed between them and nobody had bothered to warn her about it. 'Come with me,' she said.

Zahid followed her along the chilly corridor, carefully trying to avert his eyes from the rhythmic sway of her bottom and wondering why she was being so edgy. And why she was walking in a way which seemed…

They'd reached the kitchen when he worked out just what the anomaly was and he frowned. 'Is there something the matter with your hand, Francesca?'

She turned round, her heart thudding guiltily against her breast. 'My hand?'

'The one which seems to be glued to your left thigh.'

Was it rude to stand in front of a sheikh with your hand rammed deeply into your pocket? She supposed that it was. And she couldn't exactly potter one-handedly around this vast kitchen making tea, with his clever black eyes watching her, could she? Reluctantly, she withdrew her fingers, aware of the scratch of the stone against the denim and the dazzle of the gem as it emerged into the light.

The feeling of wonderment she'd been experiencing just minutes before his arrival now evaporated into one of acute embarrassment. Stupidly, she found her cheeks colouring as she lifted her eyes to meet his—but finding nothing other than cold curiosity in his gaze.

'Why, Francesca,' he said, with a note in his voice she'd never heard before. 'I don't believe it. You're engaged to be married.'

CHAPTER TWO

BLACK eyes burned into her with a question blazing at their depths and for a moment Frankie felt oddly weak beneath their fierce scrutiny.

'You're getting married?' Zahid queried silkily.

Frankie nodded, her throat parchment-dry, wondering why she was feeling so damned nervous when she should have been feeling *proud.* 'Yes. Yes, I am.'

'When did this happen?'

'Just—yesterday.'

'Let me see. Oh, please don't be coy about it.' His black eyes gleamed with some dark emotion she didn't recognise. 'Come on, Francesca—I thought that all women loved showing off their engagement rings?'

Reluctantly, Frankie extended her hand and as he took it in his she felt the prickle of awareness as the sheikh's warm flesh touched hers. Hadn't there been years and years when she'd dreamt of Zahid holding her hand like this? And yet the exquisite irony was that at last it was happening and it meant precisely nothing. All he was doing was holding her hand so that he could examine an engagement ring bought for her by another man!

Zahid frowned as he studied the gem closely, feeling her unmistakable shiver as she pulled her fingers away. And hadn't he felt the faintest whisper of something himself? Something which, if he didn't know better, might almost have been the first potent shimmering of desire. Lifting his head, he met her eyes, raising his brows in mocking query. 'But surely this should be a cause for celebration, rather than secrecy?'

The colour in her cheeks intensified. 'Oh, but it is.' *So why had she been hiding the ring from him?* The unspoken question hovered on the air, but even if he'd asked her Frankie doubted whether she would have been able to come up with a satisfactory explanation. Not to him—not even to herself. And as it happened, he didn't ask her.

'So who's the lucky man?'

'His name's Simon Forrester.'

'Simon Forrester.' Zahid pulled out a chair from beneath the large, scrubbed oak table and sat down, spreading his legs out in front of him. Idly, he noticed the unusual and fancy display of hothouse roses which were sitting there replacing the hand-picked sprigs from the garden which she normally favoured. Had 'Simon' bought her those? Was he the reason for the long hair and the junking of her glasses? The incentive to start wearing sexy jeans and a clinging sweater? Had Simon woken her up to all kinds of new experiences, as well as a new way of dressing?

Inexplicably, he felt the souring flavour of distaste in his mouth. 'And what does he do, this Simon Forrester?'

Frankie's smile became fixed. Wasn't this what she had instinctively been fearing—having to give a detailed account? She felt like telling him that it wasn't his place to just breeze in after however long it had been and start interrogating her. But she knew that there was no point. Zahid was used to getting exactly what he wanted—and why on earth *wouldn't* she tell him?

'He owns the estate agency I work in. Remember I mentioned I'd started there, in one of my Christmas cards?'

Had she? Zahid frowned. He was certain she knew that Christmas wasn't celebrated in Khayarzah, but she still insisted on sending him a card every year. And for some reason, he insisted on opening them himself—instead of letting one of his aides deal with it. They were always variations on a theme: images of robins and berry-laden sprigs of holly. Or carol singers singing in snowy villages. And even though he didn't celebrate Christmas, he did find those cards made him nostalgic for the years he spent in England while he was at boarding school.

'Maybe you did mention it,' he said slowly. But it was a surprise. Hadn't he thought she might follow a scientific route, like her father? 'Tell me more.'

Frankie bit her lip. He didn't have a clue what she was talking about! Obviously, he never even bothered to read the chatty accompanying letter she always took the time to tuck inside the annual card. 'Well, Simon runs a very successful company—'

'Not about the company, Francesca—about *him*,' he butted in. 'This man you are proposing to marry. This *Simon Forrester.*'

It wasn't easy when she felt as if he were spearing her with hostile black light from his eyes and spitting out Simon's name as if it were some particularly nasty kind of medicine, but Frankie tried to remember all the things she liked best about her fiancé. Those blue eyes and the way he'd dazzled her with his attention. The roses which he'd had sent to her house, week after week—she, who had never received a bunch of flowers in her life!

She licked her lips. 'He's not the kind of man I would have normally expected to go out with—'

'Really? You go out with many men, do you?' he fired back. 'And then compare them?'

'N-no.' Why on earth was he looking at her so *darkly*? 'That's not what I meant.'

'So what *do* you mean?'

Frankie swallowed as she filled the kettle from the big, old-fashioned sink and put it on to boil. Why was he tying her up in knots with his clever line in questioning and, furthermore, why was he being so…*aggressive*? As if he had some sort of *right* to question her. Resisting the impulse to tell him it was none of his business, she forced her mind back to Simon and an image of his face popped into her mind. She thought of the thick lock of hair which flopped onto his forehead unless he brushed it back, which he did—rather a lot, as it happened. 'Well, he's blond and *very* good-looking.'

Zahid scowled. 'I'm disappointed in you, Francesca,' he said. 'Are you really so superficial that physical attributes matter most?'

'That's rich, coming from you!' said Frankie quietly, before she could stop herself.

There was a short and disbelieving silence. 'I'm sorry?'

'It doesn't matter.'

'Oh, but it does.' His voice dipped to a tone of menacing silk. 'Tell me.'

Frankie met the flash of annoyance which sparked from his eyes. Why *shouldn't* she tell him? He didn't think twice about foisting his opinion on *her*. 'You're not such an angel your-self, are you, Zahid? Don't you use your so-called "business" trips to Europe and the United States as a cover-up for your affairs with women?'

It would have been laughable if it were not so insulting and Zahid felt a mounting fury that Francesca—whom he had known all her life—could think so poorly of him. As if he were noth-ing more than some brainless *stud*. 'And just where did you acquire this fascinating piece of information?'

'The gossip columns are always full of your exploits—though I notice that they've tailed off since you became King. But prior to that, you were always being seen with some woman or other!'

'How very naïve you are, Francesca.' With a

faint sigh of impatience, he shook his dark head and subjected her to a look of chilly censure. 'Do you really believe everything you read in the papers?'

'I believe the evidence of my own eyes! I've seen enough photos of you with…with…' To her fury and consternation, Frankie found that her breath was catching in her throat and that her mind was now being plagued with images far more vivid than that of Simon's face.

Zahid with a Hollywood hottie gazing up at him, with naked adoration on her face. Zahid being papped with a sexy international lawyer who had been representing one of his rivals in some complicated court case. Except that she was pretty sure it wasn't written into a legal code of conduct that a legal representative should look at her own client's adversary as if she'd like to eat him up for breakfast. 'With all *kinds* of women!' she finished hotly. 'Making you look like some sort of international *playboy*!'

Zahid winced and, to be fair, he conceded that she *did* have a point. He *had* always enjoyed a colourful and varied sex-life until the constraints of his unexpected new role as King had forced him to employ a little more prudence. But even so...

'And you think that's the *only* reason I travel?' he demanded. 'To have affairs with women?'

As his tone of indignation washed over her Frankie forced herself to remember all his humanitarian work. She thought about the money he'd poured into a world peace project and the well-received speeches he had made on the subject. Just because she had experienced the green-eyed monster when she'd seen the photos didn't mean that she should make him out to be some kind of uncaring brute who was only interested in bedding members of the opposite sex.

She shook her head. 'No, of course I don't and I shouldn't have implied that I did,' she said stiffly, tipping boiling water into a pot containing two mint tea bags and glancing up to find his eyes on her. 'But even you wouldn't deny that it's probably one of the perks of being away from all the restrictions in Khayarzah.'

He gave a brief nod. How well she knew him. Or maybe it was just that she was permitted the rare freedom to be able to voice such thoughts because of her long association with his family. And because of the great debt he owed to her father…

'I'm sorry about your father,' he said suddenly. 'And I'm sorry I couldn't get to the funeral.'

Frankie puckered her lips tightly as she picked up the teapot. Don't show emotion, she told herself fiercely. It's counterproductive because it will only get you upset—and it really isn't done to break down in front of the sheikh, no matter how well you think you know him.

'I understand,' she answered, her voice sounding like a child's squeaky toy. 'You explained in your letter that you had only just acceded to the throne, and that you c-couldn't get away.'

Zahid nodded, remembering back to those troubled days—when the crown he had never imagined he would wear had been placed on his head. 'I couldn't,' he said simply.

'It was good of your brother to come in your

place. And that wreath you sent,' Frankie added, with a gulp. 'It was absolutely b-beautiful.'

He heard her voice wobble and he glared, getting up from the table to take the teapot from her trembling hands. 'Here. Let me take that.'

'You can't pour your own tea.'

'Don't be so ridiculous,' he returned. 'I can just about upend a pot of boiling water. Or do you think I have people waiting on me every second of the day?'

'Pretty much.'

A faint smile edged the corners of his mouth. 'Impertinent woman,' he murmured, and as he said it found himself looking into her startled blue eyes as one word leapt out and hung in the air surrounding them. He felt a pulse of heat deep in his groin. *Woman*. He swallowed. He would never have said that to her before. Nor found himself looking at her lips and wondering what it would be like to kiss them—even though they weren't wearing a scrap of make-up. Did *Simon* not like her wearing make-up? he wondered heatedly.

Frankie took one of the mugs of tea and quickly moved away—the fact that it was burning her hand hardly noticeable when measured against the hot burning in her cheeks which had followed that curiously intense moment back then. 'I'll… I'll get some honey,' she said.

Glad to have the distraction of moving away, she walked over to one of the cupboards. Her fingers were trembling as she brought out a half-filled jar and handed it to him, and she watched as he spooned a teaspoonful of honey in each cup, seeing it melt in a golden puddle into the pale green liquid.

He looked up then, a careless question in his eyes. 'So when do I get to meet him?'

'Meet him?' Francesca's heart thudded. Surely he didn't mean what she thought he meant? 'Wh-who?'

'Simon.'

She stared at him, trying to disguise her horror—some instinct telling her that Zahid and Simon should be kept apart at all costs. 'Wh-why on earth would you want to meet him?'

He shrugged and her obvious reluctance to have him do so only fired up his sense of determination that he should. 'Why wouldn't I? My country owes a great debt to your father and I am an old family friend. Since you don't have any senior male relative to look out for you, I consider it my duty to meet the man you are intending to marry.'

Frankie hoped that her face didn't betray her appalled reaction to his suggestion—and not just because he had painted a rather grim image of himself as a "senior male relative". The last thing she wanted was for him to meet Simon—because surely Zahid would make *any* man look hapless in his presence.

'Well, perhaps we can arrange something for the next time you're in town,' she said, with the confident air of someone who knew that tight royal schedules made such casual meetings almost impossible.

'But aren't you seeing him tonight? Aren't you planning to cook him dinner?'

She wondered how on earth he could have

known that until she saw him looking at the covered dish of chicken and the little heap of potatoes waiting to be peeled; the box of unopened candles which lay next to them. Perhaps he had been a detective in another life, she thought crossly. 'Yes, I'm cooking him dinner. I'd ask you to join us except that you're probably busy.' She gave a weak smile. 'And I've only got two chicken breasts.'

Zahid almost laughed at the sheer banality of her statement, but the truth of it was that her attitude was firing him up even more. He wasn't used to people saying no to him. And his curiosity had been aroused. What was she trying to hide? 'No woman should have to cook a meal when she's just got engaged—she should be freed from the drudgery of domesticity and left to enjoy the romance,' he said silkily. 'So I'll take you and Simon out to dinner instead.'

'No, honestly—'

'Yes, *honestly*,' he mocked. 'I insist. What's the name of a good local restaurant?'

'Le Poule au Pot is pretty good—but you'll never get a table this late.'

'Please don't be naïve, Francesca—I can always get a table. I'll meet you in there at eight-thirty,' he said implacably, as—pushing away his untouched tea—he got up from the table.

Frankie scrambled to her feet, aware of the sheer power of his body as she stared up into his hawklike features. 'I suppose there's no point in me trying to change your mind?'

'No point at all.' Black eyes bored into her. 'And why would you want to?'

This silky challenge she couldn't—or wouldn't—answer. All she knew was that the thought of subjecting Simon—and herself—to the distracting company of the powerful man she'd known since childhood was filling her with trepidation.

Zahid looked down into her upturned face and those strangely kissable lips, which her tiny white teeth were currently digging into as she turned anxious blue eyes up at him. And in that moment she looked so vulnerable yet so damned *sexy* that he began to wonder whether fate might not have had a hand in bringing him here today.

'Just don't be late,' he added softly.

CHAPTER THREE

'SMILE, baby, and just relax—we're going to have a ball.'

Relax? Frankie swallowed down the acid taste of nerves as Simon eased his car into the last available spot in the Le Poule au Pot's car park. How could she possibly relax, knowing that an evening with Zahid lay ahead of them? Questions had been spinning round in her head all the time she was getting ready. Wondering why the autocratic sheikh was insisting on taking them out to dinner—and what on earth his agenda was. Was it really because he wanted to vet Simon, to see if he measured up and was suitable? And if so, wasn't that an awfully *old-fashioned* point of view?

'I just wish we weren't going out,' she said, her fingers playing nervously with her necklace.

'And having a quiet dinner at home instead—the way we'd planned.'

Simon put the brakes on and shot a quick look at himself in the driving mirror. 'Are you crazy? You're best buddies with some *sheikh*—'

'I wouldn't describe us as "best buddies"—'

'Well, friendly enough for him to invite us out. And you'd rather be sitting in your old kitchen with a home-cooked meal? I mean, what planet are you on, Frankie? *Wait* till I tell everyone that I had dinner with a royal!'

'But you mustn't,' put in Frankie anxiously. 'That's the whole point. You're not supposed to mention it to anyone—it's an infringement on their privacy and they get little enough of that as it is.'

Simon's smile was tight. 'Let's not drift too far from reality, shall we? I don't need lessons in protocol from my secretary.' He gave her knee a quick squeeze. 'Even if she does also happen to be my fiancée!'

She gave him a weak, answering smile but Frankie's heart was pounding as they entered the restaurant and she felt an overpowering feeling of relief when she realised that Zahid wasn't there. Maybe he'd changed his mind about coming, she thought hopefully as they were led to their table. Decided that something more important— or someone very beautiful—had come up. Any minute now and the maître d' would discreetly slide up to their table and tell them that he had been unavoidably detained, and…

'Hello, Francesca.'

She'd been so deep in thought that she hadn't noticed the sheikh enter the room until his silken and faintly accented voice broke into her thoughts. She looked up and there he was, standing in front of their table like some dark god—with Simon springing to his feet as if his long-lost brother had just appeared and for one awful moment Frankie thought that he was actually going to try to *embrace* the sheikh.

But Zahid pre-empted any inappropriate familiarity by extending a cool hand in greeting and an even cooler smile. 'You must be Simon.'

'And you must be Zahid. Frankie's told me *all* about you.'

'Has she really?' Dark eyes were briefly glittered in her direction as Frankie attempted to clamber to her feet, but a careless wave of his hand indicated that she should remain seated.

'Of course I haven't,' said Frankie. 'And please won't you sit down, Zahid?' she added on a whisper. 'Everyone's staring at us.'

It was true. Even the eyes of the more studiedly cool diners seemed to be drawn irresistibly to the tall man in the impeccably cut suit, whose two burly-looking companions had been seated rather ostentatiously at a table right by the door. Frankie sighed. Even if it hadn't been for his bodyguards, he just oozed power, wealth and a potent sexual charisma which had all the women in the restaurant responding to him. She could see a blonde who'd been shoehorned into a silver dress and who seemed to be wearing most of Fort Knox around her neck was now flashing him a sticky, vermilion-lipsticked smile.

But Zahid seemed oblivious to the restrained

excitement his presence was causing. Instead, he sat down with his back to the room, and as two waiters fussed round them with the kind of speed she wasn't used to Frankie realised that this was the first time she'd actually been out in public with him—and that this must be what it was like all the time. The flattery and deference. His every wish anticipated and granted. No wonder his manner could be so assured and so…so…*arrogant.*

Having refused wine himself, Zahid ordered champagne for a clearly eager Simon and then leaned back in his chair—looking, thought Frankie indignantly, as if he were interviewing them for some sort of job!

'I gather congratulations are in order, Simon,' he murmured. 'You are indeed a lucky man.'

Simon took a mouthful of champagne, followed by an appreciative glance at the label on the bottle. 'Aren't I just? Although naturally, there were lots of raised eyebrows when we first announced it!'

Zahid slowly curled his fingers over the

starched linen surface of the tablecloth. 'Really?' he questioned coolly.

Simon leaned across the table towards him, in a man-to-man kind of way. 'Well, lots of my friends were surprised to begin with,' he confided.

Frankie squirmed. She could guess what was coming and although she didn't usually mind Simon's justifiable boasts about the dramatic effect he'd had on her appearance, something in her rebelled at having *Zahid* hear them. 'Zahid isn't interested,' she said quickly.

'Oh, but Zahid is,' corrected the sheikh archly. 'In fact, he's absolutely fascinated. Do continue, Simon.'

Simon gave a disarming shrug. 'Well, Frankie isn't my usual type. In fact, she won't mind me saying that she looked a bit of a geek when she came to work for me, didn't you, darling?' He shrugged like a man who had found a winning lottery ticket scrunched up on the pavement. 'So I told her to grow her hair, to lose the glasses and wear a few clothes that might show off her body—and suddenly it's "Good Morning, Cinderella!".' He raked the flop of blond hair off his forehead and glittered her the kind of smile which had once made her go weak at the knees. 'And just look at her now!'

Zahid turned his head, taking in the slump of Francesca's shoulders and the look of acute embarrassment on her face. And even though he had been amazed and surprised by her new look, he would not have dreamed of speaking of it in such a way. He certainly would not have boasted about it as if he had been preparing a horse for its first important race. A slow tide of rage began to build up inside him. What kind of a man had she harnessed her destiny to—who would humiliate her in such a way? Some pretty-pretty blond boy who was drinking champagne as if it were cordial!

'Why, you flaunt her as if she were a new toy,' he observed softly.

'And a very cuddly toy she is, too,' said Simon.

Frankie knew Zahid well enough to know when he was angry and he was very angry now.

Surely Simon wasn't blind to the nerve which was flickering at his temple, or the way he had started flexing and unflexing his long fingers on the starchy linen tablecloth. Why wouldn't he shut up? Her eyes were beseeching him to stop being indiscreet but he didn't even notice her—instead he seemed transfixed by his royal dining companion.

'Shall we…order?' she questioned hurriedly.

'Yeah, let's.' Simon scanned the menu with the avaricious scrutiny of someone who knew they wouldn't be paying the bill. 'I'll have the foie gras, followed by the duck à l'orange.'

Across the table, Zahid's black eyes met hers and she thought she read in them a mixture of mockery and contempt. She felt like squirming in her seat—or trying to explain that Simon wasn't *always* like this—but instead she just offered the sheikh a polite smile.

'Francesca?' he questioned sardonically.

She wasn't in the least bit hungry, but she could hardly sit there with an empty plate while her fiancé ate his way through a gourmet feast. 'Oh, a salad—and then the fish please.'

'I'll have the same,' said Zahid, snapping shut his leather menu and handing it back to the maître d'. 'I'm assuming you'll drink wine, Simon?'

'Love to!' Simon beamed. 'Frankie can drive, can't you, darling?'

'Of course I can.'

The drinks and first courses were brought and after he'd seen off most of his foie gras, Simon, now further emboldened by more wine, pushed back his lock of blond hair and smiled at Zahid.

'I'm still not entirely sure how you happen to be such a good friend of the family, Zahid,' he said. 'Something to do with your fathers being friends, isn't it?'

Zahid nodded. There was no earthly reason not to try to engage in conversation with the man—even though something about him was setting his teeth on edge. He glanced over at Francesca, who was picking uninterestedly at a plate of salad, and he found his eyes lingering with reluctant fascination on the creamy swell of her breasts, which was emphasised by the silky black dress she wore.

Swallowing down the sudden stir of lust, he looked at Simon. 'Our fathers were indeed friends—they met at university and maintained that connection throughout their lives. You know that Francesca's father was a geologist?'

'Well, I never met him, of course,' said Simon. 'He sounds as if he was brilliant.' He smirked. 'Though more than a bit batty—a sort of nutty-professor type.'

Francesca looked up, her face flushing. 'Eccentric,' she corrected. 'He was eccentric.'

'He was very brilliant,' said Zahid icily. 'It was through his ground-breaking work into unusual rock formations in the desert that we discovered Khayarzah's first oil well. That discovery brought unimaginable riches to my country at a time when they were badly needed.' His eyes met Francesca's and he held her gaze, giving her a soft smile. 'Leaving us for ever indebted to him.'

Simon swirled some ruby-coloured claret in his glass and took a large mouthful. 'Ah, so that explains why your father gifted him the house and land,' he said smoothly.

Zahid arched questioning eyebrows at Francesca and she rushed in with an explanation—terrified he would think she'd been abusing their friendship by blabbing or boasting about it.

'Simon couldn't work out why we had such a big property in such a wealthy area and no…'

'No money!' finished Simon cheerfully. 'I'm afraid that Frankie is asset rich and cash poor, as we say in the business. It's a common enough scenario—and completely unnecessary, especially when she's sitting on an absolute gold mine. Land round here is worth an absolute fortune—which is why we're putting the house on the market as soon as possible.'

There was an odd kind of pause and when Frankie looked into Zahid's eyes she didn't like what she could see there. Was that disappointment she could read?

'You're selling the house?' he asked quietly.

'It's so big,' she said helplessly, wishing he wouldn't look at her so *disapprovingly*.

'But you love that house, Francesca.'

She bit her lip. Of course she loved it—who wouldn't love it? Much of her past was tied up in the place. It was a very old and beautiful building with a disused laboratory in the grounds, where her father used to work. It also had large and exquisitely laid-out grounds, which looked glorious during every season of the year. But she couldn't afford the upkeep and the garden was much too big for one person to handle—and Simon was unwilling to take it on.

'And it's so expensive to maintain,' she added, though Zahid's grim expression did not soften one bit.

Simon nodded. 'Life will be much easier without it. I've told her that if we give the place a lick of paint and stick a few hanging baskets outside, then we should be able to shift it fairly quickly.' He fiddled with the signet ring on his little finger and winked at Frankie. 'And then we'll be able to move into one of the brand-new houses which are being built in the middle of town. Perfect for us, aren't they, darling?'

'You seem to have it all planned out, Simon,' said Zahid slowly.

Simon nodded. 'You could say that I needed to. Frankie has her head in the clouds a lot of the time—she just needs a little guidance, that's all.'

'And you feel you are just the person to do it, do you?'

'As her fiancé, yes, I do.'

Frankie cringed. She felt like an outsider as she sat there, picking at her food and listening to the two men engaged in an unmistakable sparring match. Zahid was interrogating Simon as if he were a suspect in some major crime and Simon was showing off—it was as simple as that.

It was a strange sensation watching them both—as if she were a spectator at some sort of gladiatorial event. But worse than that, it seemed as if Zahid were holding up a mirror and she was suddenly seeing Simon through *his* eyes.

Her blond fiancé's breezy confidence—which had once so captivated her—now appeared to be more like a conceited swagger. Was that co-incidence, she wondered—or was Zahid delib-erately winding him up? Needling him with all the wrong questions in order to make him look bad.

But why on earth would he do something like that?

Not that she cared what Zahid's motives were—they, and he, were irrelevant to her life. She *loved* Simon. He was the first real boyfriend she'd ever had—when she'd given up hope of ever finding anyone who cared about her. Hadn't he stepped into her life when she'd most needed someone? Given her a job even though she wasn't really qualified for anything, because she'd spent much of the last few years looking after her sick father. And he'd given her so much more than that, hadn't he? He'd offered her a glimpse of what a normal life could be like—with pubs and restaurants and trips to the cinema. He'd changed her from the geeky young woman who had walked so hesitantly into his life and made her into someone he wasn't ashamed to be seen with. She'd been so grateful for that…grateful to *him*.

Refusing pudding and the brandy which Simon accepted with alacrity, Frankie was relieved when at last the dinner was over and it was time to leave—though she noticed that they weren't presented with anything as vulgar as a bill. She saw one of the bodyguards speaking to the maître d' and assumed that he had dealt with the financial transaction.

'Th-thanks very much, Zahid,' said Simon as he rose unsteadily to his feet.

But the sheikh's attention was focused solely on Frankie. 'You're sure you're going to be okay getting home?' he questioned, with a frown.

'I've only had water all night,' she said.

'It's dark. I can have one of my aides drive the car for you?'

She smiled. How old-fashioned he could be! 'I'm perfectly capable of driving home, thank you, Zahid—and I'm fine in the dark. My eyesight is perfect and it's only just down the road!'

But Zahid wasn't happy. Not happy at all. He

watched while Francesca was handed her coat by the cloakroom attendant. It was a cheap-looking thing, in his opinion—and as she slid it over her shoulders it covered up the milky-pale flesh of her arms, which had drawn his eye throughout the meal.

Would Simon be removing the coat and then the dress later? he wondered—and a spear of some unknown emotion shot through him. It made his blood feel thick and his groin heavy. It felt like desire but it was underpinned with something else. Something dark and bitter and unpalatable. Surely… He shook his head. Surely it wasn't *jealousy*? Why on earth would he be jealous of little Francesca O'Hara's lover—when he could have any woman he wanted?

Except that she wasn't so little any more, was she? Not in any sense. Not in height, or… He swallowed. Surely the last time he'd seen her, she'd been completely flat-chested? Or had the slouchy clothes she used to favour done her *no* favours?

'Thanks so much for the meal, Zahid.'

She was smiling up at him now—the curve of her lips putting deep dimples in her cheeks the way it had done all those years ago, and he was hit by a renewed wave of protectiveness.

He found himself remembering the time when, as a lively ten-year-old, she had scrambled into a huge tree looking for a lost shuttlecock and managed to get herself stranded there. He had climbed up into the branches and rescued her, quietening her teeth-chattering fear with a few teasing words of admonishment. And she had put her arms around his neck and clung to him like a little monkey.

He should have been there for her when her father had died. Why the hell hadn't his brother reported back to him that she was vulnerable? And she *was* vulnerable. Even now. Anyone could see that.

He saw Simon giving a young waitress an easy smile, the careless crinkling of his eyes the tell-tale sign of the practised flirt. But Francesca didn't seem to have noticed.

Zahid watched as she buttoned up her thin

coat, the ostentatious engagement ring glittering on her finger, and his mouth tightened. A man would have to spend a lot of money to buy a diamond that size, he thought suddenly. A man who was a lot more committed than her pretty-boy fiancé seemed to be.

'You're going back home soon, are you, Zahid?' Francesca was asking.

She was leaning towards him and he caught an elusive drift of her scent—which smelt of rain-washed rose petals—and a distracting shiver began to whisper its way over his skin.

'Mmm?' he questioned distractedly.

She dimpled him another smile. 'I feel so guilty—we've hardly said a word about you all evening, and I love hearing about Khayarzah.'

'Please don't feel guilty,' said Zahid as he nodded over at one of his bodyguards to indicate that they were ready to leave. 'We shall be meeting very soon and I will tell you everything you wish to know.'

Frankie smiled uncertainly. Was he just making polite conversation? Unlikely. Yet they both knew how uncommon his visits to England were, especially these days. But suddenly, she could see that it was probably a good thing that their paths didn't cross very often. Too much of Zahid Al Hakam could make a woman feel very discontented with her lot. 'What, you mean next year?' she joked.

'No, not next year, but next week,' he corrected silkily. 'I have business in mainland Europe all this week—but after that, I'll come back.'

'Come back?' questioned Frankie nervously, turning her head to look for Simon and wondering what that waitress could be saying to him, which was making him look so engrossed. 'Come back where?'

'Don't look so scared, Francesca—I just meant that we still have a lot of catching up to do.' Zahid's eyes flicked over to Simon, who was now leaning even closer to the young waitress. 'I'm sure your fiancé won't object if I visit you again on my return.'

Like a goldfish, Frankie opened her mouth and shut it again. Because how could she possibly object? Even if Zahid hadn't been a king whose requests could not be turned down from a protocol point of view—she could hardly tell him that she thought it was a bad idea, because she found him dangerous and unsettling as a man. Why, he would probably laugh in her face.

So she nodded obediently and hoped her misgivings didn't show. 'Okay. I'll…I'll look forward to it.'

'So will I,' promised Zahid softly.

CHAPTER FOUR

IN THE days which followed the awkward restaurant meal Frankie tried to convince herself that the sheikh's promise to return must have been made on the spur of the moment. He probably hadn't meant it. It was the kind of flippant thing which people always said when they were leaving—"oh, we must meet up soon"—and then you didn't see them for years.

But she was wrong. One of his aides rang and told her that he would be arriving on Saturday afternoon and that he wished to see her, alone.

Alone?

Uncomfortably, she touched her shiny new engagement ring—as if expecting it to suddenly disappear in a puff of smoke. Her conscience was making her feel slightly awkward and she had been worried what Simon would say. Was it

wrong for her to have made an arrangement to
see the king?

Nervously, she'd asked her fiancé about
Zahid's proposed visit, but it seemed that Simon
didn't mind at all. In fact, to Frankie's surprise
he seemed inordinately pleased by the idea.

'Maybe he's planning to give you a wedding
present—hopefully in the form of some whack-
ing great cheque,' he said, when she told him.

'That's a very mercenary thing to say,' objected
Frankie.

'I'm a businessman, sweetheart—being mercenary goes with the territory!' He fiddled with his
gold signet ring and shot her a sly glance. 'Maybe
you could get him to invest in some property
while you're at it? That colossal eyesore at the
top of the hill could do with a big injection of
Middle Eastern cash.'

'I don't think so.' With a wan smile, she walked
out of Simon's office, wishing that she could
shrug off the restlessness which had haunted her
since the night they'd had dinner with Zahid. Up
until that point, she had been relatively contented

with her lot. She'd been anticipating being a new wife, with a new life ahead of her—but now everything had changed and, deep down, she knew exactly why. It was all because she had seen the dashing desert king again, after years of absence.

Images of his hawklike features kept flashing into her mind at the most inopportune moments. She had found herself filling up her car at the petrol station and wondering if Khayarzah might have supplied the fuel. Last night she'd even dreamt about him—some stupid, school-girlish fantasy which seemed to involve him riding in the desert on one of his favoured black stallions and scooping her into the saddle in front of him…

And this morning she had woken up with her heart racing and an odd, squirmy feeling at the pit of her stomach—plus a terrible feeling of guilt that she could feel that way about him, when she was planning to marry Simon.

She prepared for Zahid's visit with the same care she'd employed when she'd been growing up and he and his father used to stop by. Nowadays she was rather more efficient at cleaning the house, and the home-made cake which filled the kitchen with the smell of lemons didn't have a great big crater in the centre.

The pale roses which Simon had bought were already dead and so Frankie put on her old raincoat and went outside to look for something to replace them. Although she hadn't dared tell her fiancé, she much preferred home-grown flowers to the forced, hothouse variety—and you could always find something suitable which was already growing in the garden.

Especially *this* garden, she thought as she looked around and breathed in the damp, autumnal air. How she loved this garden—and how she would miss it when she moved into the town house which Simon had his eye on, where they all had nothing but a small, paved 'easy-care' patio area.

The misty atmosphere of the November day had created diamonds on the cobwebs and fallen leaves lay like scattered toffee wrappers on the wet grass. Taking out her pair of secateurs, she began to snip at some of the hips and berry laden branches and soon her basket was half-full. She would cram them in that big copper pot and the dark green foliage and scarlet berries would contrast against it quite perfectly and brighten up the kitchen.

The sound of a powerful engine disturbed her thoughts and, turning round, she saw Zahid's sports car growling its way up the drive before coming to a halt next to her own, rather beaten-up old car.

Frankie watched as he got out—and once again she was reminded of his chameleon-like capacity. Today's look was casual and expensive and very, very compelling. Faded blue jeans clung to his powerful legs and beneath his leather jacket she could see a dark cashmere sweater, which echoed the coal-black of his hair. She let her gaze linger on his stern expression and her heart gave a curious little flutter before her fingers curled tightly around the secateurs she was holding. What kind of a disloyal and horrible woman was she, if the sight of a man who wasn't her fiancé should fill her with an overwhelming sense of excitement? What was the *matter* with her?

Putting her basket down, she went across the damp grass to meet him, her smile feeling forced. 'Hello, Zahid.'

'Francesca.' He looked down at her, thinking how young and *innocent* she looked today. And much more like the Francesca he knew of old, with that big old raincoat and a pair of wellington boots which had seen better days. But the dark, mist-sprinkled hair still hung in a silken fall over her shoulders and her eyes were still that newly discovered shade of blue. And she was no longer young, he thought grimly. Nor innocent. He felt an odd twist of his heart and a sense of anger building inside him, but he forced himself to control it. 'Has Simon recovered after the other night?'

'Yes, he was fine. Had a bit of a headache the next day. He says to say thank you for dinner— and hopes he wasn't out of order.'

Black eyes bored into her. 'Does he always drink that much?'

'Of course he doesn't!' She saw the look of censure on his face and wondered why he had to be so judgemental—had *he* never had a few drinks too many? She supposed he hadn't—for none of the Al Hakam family drank alcohol, did they? 'He was probably just nervous, meeting you. You must be used to that, Zahid—it's not every day that someone like Simon gets to have dinner with a real-live sheikh.'

'Maybe not—but it was naïve and inappropriate behaviour in the circumstances. Especially for a man of—*how* old is he, Francesca?'

'He's twenty-eight—he's hardly about to start drawing his pension!' Frankie frowned when he gave no answering smile. 'Have you come here today just to talk about Simon?'

'Actually, yes. I have.'

She stared at him. 'Well, if we're talking inappropriate—then wanting to discuss my fiancé with me behind his back surely falls into that category? Okay, so he *got a little drunk*—big deal! These things happen sometimes—they probably happen in Khayarzah, if you only knew it!'

'But nobody there would dare to get drunk in front of the king!' Zahid snapped, before drawing in a deep breath, reminding himself that he had come here today with a purpose. Not a particularly palatable one, it was true—but he needed to muster up every diplomatic atom in his body if he was to limit the emotional damage his discovery was going to have on Francesca. 'Shall we take a walk around the garden?'

At this, she smiled. 'Are you sure you wouldn't prefer to go inside, into the warmth? I've made you a cake.'

He felt the unfamiliar stab of guilt. She'd spent the morning making him a cake—just like old times. While he had spent the morning accruing information which would…

'No cake, thank you.' He saw the brief look of hurt which flitted over her pale face and forced himself to breathe out a platitude. 'I'm sorry if you went to any trouble.'

'Not even your favourite lemon?'

'Francesca—' He paused, reluctant to open the

can of grotesquely wriggling worms he was in possession of. 'Tell me how you met Simon.'

'Oh, for heaven's sake.' Couldn't he let this go? 'Does it really matter?'

'Yes.' His gaze was steady. 'It matters a lot.'

She stared at him, remembering about what he'd said the other day. Something about it being his 'duty' to meet Simon. And if that was the case, then wasn't he taking duty a little too far? 'Is this another quasi-paternal question?' she questioned.

Paternal? Zahid winced. God help him but he didn't feel in the least bit paternal at the moment—not when those wide-spaced eyes looked so blue and so deep that he felt he might be able to dive into them. 'Just answer the question,' he said unevenly.

She sighed, giving into the inevitable—sensing that he wouldn't give her any peace until she provided him with the information he wanted. 'I met him when he came to the house after my father died.'

Zahid nodded. 'So he knew your father? He came to pay his respects?'

Francesca bit her lip because the next piece of information had never sat very easily with her—even when Simon had explained that people in the business world needed to be outgoing in order to keep themselves afloat.

'Not really,' she said slowly. 'He'd read about his death in the papers and so he came...he came...'

'He came to see whether you needed to sell the house?'

Frankie flushed under the black glare of his fierce scrutiny. 'I suppose so.'

'Like some low-life lawyer chasing an ambulance, touting for business?' The words were out before he could stop them.

Frankie froze. 'Don't you *dare* judge him! How would you know what it's like, Zahid? You're a sheikh and even when your country was broke, you still lived in a palace and had servants all over the place—while Simon has had to fight to make his way in the world!'

'My heart bleeds for him.'

Something about the way he said it made a queer kind of frustration bubble up inside her and for a moment Frankie actually took an angry step towards him, until he halted her with a voice like ice.

'I think you forget yourself!' he snapped. 'I allow you the kind of leeway which I wouldn't tolerate from anyone else, Francesca—but there really are limits.'

'What, so you think you can stand there and insult my fiancé and I'm just expected to take it?'

His eyes lanced her a piercing question. 'You aren't even interested why I've brought the subject up?'

Something in the way he asked it unsettled her enough to hide behind defiance. 'To cause trouble?'

'Funnily enough, my schedule is usually too tight to indulge myself with random acts of interference—especially towards people I care about.

I want you to tell me what happened next—after Simon came to see you that first time.'

Frankie was tempted not to reply—or to change the subject completely. But if she had nothing to hide, then why should she shy away from his questioning, no matter how intrusive it seemed? 'I told him that I didn't really want to sell the house unless it was absolutely necessary, and that I needed a job.'

Zahid nodded. 'So he gave you a job, a make-over and a proposal in quick succession and when you agreed to marry him, he somehow persuaded you that it was in your best interests to sell the house?'

Frankie flushed to the roots of her hair. He was making it all sound so…so *mercenary*. As if Simon had *planned* it all. 'These things happen.'

'I bet they do,' he drawled. 'But I'm right, aren't I?'

'Yes, Zahid—I expect you're always right.'

'And you don't think it's slightly suspect behaviour?'

'Why should I? Maybe I'm not as suspicious as

you are! Maybe I like to think the best of people! And Simon loves me!'

'Does he?'

Frankie stilled as something in his sombre tone iced her skin with a terrible sense of foreboding. 'Of course he does.'

'How *much* do you think he loves you?'

'What kind of a question is that?' She eyed him warily. 'Enough to want to marry me.'

There was, he realised, no diplomatic way to do this. No way of telling her which wasn't going to hurt her. 'I wonder,' he said quietly.

'Will you please stop talking in riddles? What do you wonder?'

There was another pause. Like the split-second pause before a marksman fired a bullet from a gun. And then he spoke. 'He's got another woman.'

Frankie's heart began to pound. 'What did you say?' she whispered.

'Simon's got another woman. There's someone else.'

She shook her head, her fingers flying to her cheeks. 'No! You're making it up!'

'Why would I do that?'

'I don't *know*!'

Her face had gone completely white and she swayed so that Zahid's hand automatically went out to steady her, his body tensing. Had he been so brutal with the facts that she was about to faint? Wasn't he supposed to have been diplomatic? Protective? Surely there was a way he could have told her which wouldn't have made her face looked so bleached and transparent.

Uttering a short curse in his native tongue, he bent and scooped his arms underneath her knees, despite her ineffectual protests to push him away. And as the firmness of her young body imprinted itself on his mind he was aware of the blood in his own veins growing hot and heavy. He could feel the curved definition of her thighs beneath his fingers, the soft weight of her breast as she slumped against his chest—and he felt a wave of guilty pleasure as he carried her into the house.

Some of her strength must have returned because by the time he had deposited her on the old sofa in the sitting room, she had begun half-heartedly punching against his chest—and he let her. He crouched down in front of her, holding his palms up in front of him—like a man trying to quieten a fractious horse. 'Francesca—'

Her hands fell like stones into her lap. 'Go away!' she whispered.

'You don't want the truth?'

'It isn't true! Why would he want someone else when he's engaged to me?' *But mightn't that explain why Simon had been so unbelievably cautious about making love to her? Was it really nothing to do with respect for the old-fashioned morals she'd been brought up to believe in? Had the truth of it been that all along he had another woman and didn't find Frankie attractive after all—makeover or no makeover?*

'You want proof?' he demanded.

Recovering some of her composure, Frankie sat up. 'Yes, I want proof! Except you probably haven't got any, have you? This is all because he

got a bit drunk and you're making a value judgement because you don't think he's good enough
for me!'

'Damned right he's not,' he said grimly, rising
to his feet and going outside to retrieve a package
from the passenger seat of his car, before carrying it back inside—still hoping that she might
have changed her mind and just take his word for
it. But one look at her face when he returned—a
mutinous expression written on it that he'd never
seen before—and Zahid knew that there was no
alternative but to show her.

Reluctantly, he pulled out a series of black and
white photos and silently handed them to her.

With fingers which felt frozen and a heart
which was numb, Frankie looked down at the
glossy images in her hands.

There was Simon, locking his car—an innocent enough shot, but if she looked a bit more
closely Frankie could see someone standing in
the doorway of a house, waving to him. A rangy
blonde wearing one of those skirts which only
just about covered her knickers.

The next image showed Simon warmly embracing the same woman and Frankie sought refuge in yet more denial.

'She might just be his sister, or a relative,' she croaked.

'Really?' questioned Zahid as she pulled out the third photo. 'Pretty close family, if that's the case.'

This one was the killer. There could be no mistake or misunderstanding about a close-up where Simon appeared to be going for a new world record in how much tongue it was possible to shove down a woman's throat. Frankie shuddered with revulsion as she compared it to all the chaste kisses he used to share with her. But didn't it all make sense now? The reason he'd never touched her had not been because he'd *respected* her—but because he had someone else. Someone he really cared for and desired—rather than someone he just wanted to milk for all she was worth.

With a ragged little cry, she let the photos slip

from her fingers, her hurt and dismay making her turn on Zahid.

'You had him followed!' she accused as she felt hot tears of humiliation fill her eyes. 'What right did you have to do that?'

'Francesca,' he admonished softly. 'Aren't you turning your anger on the wrong person here? I did it for your own good.'

'B-but *why*?' Frankie sobbed. 'Why did you do it? Couldn't you have just let me be happy for a while?' she cried as tears of humiliation and shame began to slide down her cheeks.

'You really think you can be happy in a relationship which is based on a tissue of lies? And then what?' he flared, when still she didn't answer. And for a moment, he acknowledged the irony of *him* dishing out advice on relationships. 'You'd have discovered even further down the line how duplicitous he was being—and found yourself even *more* hurt! Is that what you want from your life, Francesca?'

What kind of a question was that to ask her at a time like this? Scrambling to her feet, she pushed him away, her thoughts spinning round and round. But some small and stupid hope was still flickering in her heart, stubbornly refusing to be extinguished. Maybe there was some kind of explanation for it, after all. Something which Simon would explain and then she could turn round to Zahid and tell him that for once in his life he'd been *wrong*! 'I'm going to ask him!'

He shook his head. 'Don't even think about it,' he warned her grimly. 'You'll only regret it.'

But she turned on him—and part of her terrible pain was that Zahid should have borne witness to her humiliation. The man she had idolised for all her life should have seen her made a complete fool of. *That* she regretted.

'So if it's true—and we haven't even established that it is—you think I should just walk away and let him get away with it? Just fade away into the background as if I never really existed and let him get away with making a fool of me?' she raged as a sense of justice and determination began to replace her hurt and mortification.

In that moment she realised that there was going to be no mistake. That the photos told the truth and that Simon had lied to her—but one thing she was sure of was that she was not going to be some sad little *victim*. Especially in Zahid's eyes. 'Obviously, I no longer have a job—so I might as well tell him exactly what I think of him.'

'The job doesn't matter, Francesca,' he grated.

'You don't think so? Well, it might just interest you to know that I need to earn money because I need to eat! Most people do.'

He gave an impatient wave of his hand. 'I can find you a job in the flicker of an eye. I can create some sort of role for you in my organisation and it can be as permanent or as temporary as you like.'

There was a pin-drop silence as Frankie stared at him. What, and make her detachment from reality complete? She could just imagine the hawklike eye he would keep on her if she got involved with his organisation. Governed and bossed around by a powerful man who seemed to have the misplaced idea that his role was to protect her. Long ago, she had abandoned her foolish romantic dreams about him, but wouldn't enforced proximity and hurt pride make her vulnerable to him again?

She would have to watch from the sidelines while he bedded the glamorous women who were his girlfriends—and how would *that* feel? There would be all the disadvantages of being closeted with the devastatingly attractive sheikh—but none of the benefits. She would end up feeling completely invisible because to him she was just Francesca—sexless, safe Francesca who had got herself into a laughable situation with a worthless man and now needed rescuing.

'Thank you, but no, thank you,' she said tightly, walking over to the table and grabbing her shoulder bag. 'I don't know what I'm going to do with my future—but before I make any decisions, I'm going to ask Simon Forrester a few questions!'

As he watched her pull the bag over one slender shoulder Zahid knew that he could have restrained her in an instant—and not by confiscating her car keys. For wasn't there an urgent part of him which wanted to subdue her into forgetting about that worthless creep by simply *kissing* her? He felt the heavy throb of desire as arrogance and a justifiable pride in his methods of seduction told him that he would have succeeded within seconds. He could show her what it was like to be with a *real* man.

But deep down he knew that would be wrong. For all kinds of reasons, Francesca O'Hara was not a woman he was ever going to be able to seduce—and ultimately she was free to do what she needed to do. And it seemed that she needed to go and confront the man who had betrayed her.

A faint smile of admiration curved the edges of his lips as he heard the front door slamming shut behind her, and soon after that came the sound of her old car spluttering into life.

CHAPTER FIVE

'His Royal Highness, the Sheikh Zahid will see you now, Miss O'Hara.' The sleek receptionist indicated the discreet private elevator which was set in the marbled foyer of the luxury hotel. 'If you'd like to go up?'

'Thanks very much.' With a polite smile at the glacial beauty who was the last barrier between her and Zahid, Frankie walked over to the elevator and pressed the button up to the penthouse suite.

Outwardly, she was trying to project a calm and unruffled image, which wasn't easy, given her rain-swept appearance.

It had been quite an afternoon.

Tracking Zahid down hadn't been easy. It had come as something of a shock to realise that she had never actually contacted *him* before. He had mostly only visited with his father—and everything had always been arranged by palace aides. But she knew that his family owned a skyscraper headquarters in a swish central London location, where his brother masterminded the European arm of the Al Hakams' extensive empire.

Eventually, after she had spoken to a series of suspicious-sounding people who presumably okayed it with Zahid himself, an appointment had been made for her to see him. But instead of it being at the company headquarters, they'd given her the name of the hotel where he was staying. The famous Granchester hotel—the kind of place you only read about in the gossip columns of newspapers, or when a Hollywood superstar happened to be visiting town.

The elevator was so speedy that it made her feel a bit sick and Frankie couldn't help but notice that her legs were splashed with icy water from the grim November day. She dabbed at them with a tissue pulled from her bag, but by the time the elevator slid to a halt and she rapped on the door of Zahid's suite she felt even more chewed up with nerves. A feeling which was only increased when she heard his distinctive voice call: "Come!"

Her heart was pounding as she pushed open the door and for a moment she noticed nothing other than the fabulous works of art which lined the walls and the enormous windows overlooking some of the most expensive real estate in the world. The polished floor was as big as a football pitch and strewn with exquisite silken rugs. It was, she realised, the first time that she had ever been in *his* environment, and it was even more polished and intimidating than she'd thought it would be.

And now, walking in from a room which led off the main living area, came Zahid himself—his face unsmiling and not particularly welcoming as he looked at her. Was he angry that she had flung his job offer back in his face the other day? she wondered.

'Hello, Francesca,' he said. His narrowed black eyes were shuttered as he looked at her—taking in the raindrops which glittered like diamonds among the tousled strands of her dark hair. 'You'd better take off your raincoat.'

Frankie saw that she was dripping rain onto the polished wood floor and so she struggled out of her coat, wondering if he might help her. But he simply watched as she removed it and then pointed to a coat-stand which stood next to the door. She cleared her throat as she looped the damp garment over the peg then turned round to face him. 'It was good of you to see me, Zahid.'

There was the faintest elevation of his jet-dark brows. 'I was surprised you wanted to—in view of our last meeting.'

She supposed she deserved that, just as she supposed he deserved an apology for the way she'd reacted to what he told her. Was that why he was being so cool towards her? So *distant*? 'I was very…rude to you.'

He shrugged as if it didn't matter, but, of course, it did—just not in the way she thought. In a funny sort of way he had been glad about her rudeness—because hadn't it stopped him from ringing her to find out what had happened after she'd gone to confront Simon? He'd convinced himself that it would have been all about self-interest if he'd done so. And told himself that he should stay away from her—for both their sakes. Yes, he had opened her eyes to the fact that she had been involved with some pathetic fortune-hunter—but now that she was presumably free of him, it should have no impact on *his* life.

Because hadn't he been disturbed by the rush of lust he'd felt while carrying her into the house? And hadn't the thoughts he'd had about her subsequently made him realise that she had grown up into a subtle kind of beauty—and that it would be better for both of them if he kept his distance from her? Wasn't that the reason why he hadn't helped her with her coat, because he was reluctant to be tempted by her soft scent and even softer skin?

'Don't worry about your rudeness, Francesca—it's forgotten,' he said coolly. 'I probably would have felt exactly the same if the situation had been reversed.'

She watched as he walked across the room.

She wanted to protest that such a scenario would never have happened—that Zahid was far too clever to be manipulated as she had been. But somehow the words dried in her throat and it was nothing to do with their relevance. No, it was the sight of him looking like some lithe jungle cat who seemed a little too *elemental* to be at home in these luxurious surroundings.

A silk shirt of palest ivory briefly brushed against the hard contours of his torso and clung like cream to the powerful line of his shoulders. Black trousers hugged at the narrow line of his hips and skated over the cradle of his masculinity. He had loosened his tie and a couple of buttons of his shirt and, catching a glimpse of the dark hair which was arrowing downwards, she felt her mouth dry.

He looked as if he had been engrossed in work and was now relaxing a little. It was a snapshot image of his own, private world—and even more daunting than his physical appearance was the realisation that Zahid had a complete and busy life of which she knew nothing. What was it like being a king? she wondered. Particularly if such a daunting office had been thrust on you out of the blue, as had happened to him. Had it changed him? It *must* have changed him.

Frankie licked the parchment-dry surface of her lips, trying to concentrate on reality, rather than hopeless fantasy. That was yet another great difference between them, she thought. He had a life, and she didn't. Well, not any more—no job, a broken engagement and some broken dreams as well.

He slanted her a questioning look. 'Why don't you sit down, Francesca? Would you like some coffee? Or tea, perhaps?'

'No. No, thanks.' Sitting down felt too relaxed, too informal for what she was about to say—and so Frankie walked over to the massive windows on the pretext of enjoying the view. And for a moment, she didn't have to pretend. There was the London Eye—its massive circle framing the Houses of Parliament and iconic clock-face of Big Ben. 'Oh, wow,' she said.

'Picture-postcard stuff, isn't it?' he offered

drily, looking at the stiff set of her shoulders and the hair which today was hanging neatly down her back. Her hand was bare of an engagement ring and she was wearing a navy dress which, despite its plainness, still managed to emphasise every amazing curve of her healthy young body. His eyes focused on the luscious swell of her bottom and her long, shapely legs and he found himself thinking some dark and very erotic thoughts until he reminded himself that this was Francesca. Francesca O'Hara, his childhood friend.

'So is this a social call?' he questioned thickly.

She turned around. Was that his way of saying that he was busy? That he might have sat and drunk tea on *her* territory many times, but on his she was only permitted a very small window in his own busy schedule.

'No. It's not.' He was staring at her, not saying anything, and once again she felt frozen out. Gone was the ease which had always existed between them, even during that last, emotionally charged meeting.

She had thought that he'd be eager to hear about her confrontation with Simon. But she had been wrong. There had been no phone call to ask what had happened and even now, face to face, there was only a polite indifference as to why she had come today. Here in the luxury hotel suite, she was simply someone from his past. The daughter of an old friend—in the presence of a very powerful, royal personage. And she was probably *wasting his time*.

'So if it isn't *social*, then why exactly are you here?' he queried coolly.

For a moment she felt tempted to make some lame excuse and to walk away, leaving her with her dignity intact and not running the risk of him saying no to what she was going to ask him. Wouldn't that be easier?

But wasn't it exactly that kind of grabbing at the easy option which had made it laughingly simple for Simon to make a fool of her?

'I was wondering if I could take you up on that offer you made?' She noticed that his body had tensed and her words stumbled over themselves to give him a reasonable get-out clause. 'You… you mentioned something about giving me a role within your organisation. But if you've changed your mind, then I quite understand.'

'It's you who seems to have changed your mind, Francesca—since you were adamant that you didn't want any kind of role in my organisation,' he returned silkily. 'Would you care to tell me why?'

She swallowed. It was hateful having to relive scenes she'd sooner forget—and more than a little disappointing that Zahid should have asked her for some sort of explanation. Had she thought that instantly he would become malleable and go along with her wishes as he had done when she'd been growing up? But she was no longer asking him to carry her around on his shoulders or rescue her shuttlecock from the branches of a tree. She needed a far more grown-up favour from him than that.

'I went to see Simon—and he…' Briefly, Frankie closed her eyes as she remembered the ugly showdown. Simon's initial blustering denial and then his sneer when he realised he was cornered. He'd said a few things she would never forget—about the fact that she was about as alluring as a plate of cold porridge and it had been no hardship not to bed her. He told her she was a fool if she thought that Zahid having him followed meant anything other than that the sheikh was an interfering control freak. And that she certainly shouldn't start reading anything into it. That a man like that might play with her for a while and then discard her like last year's calendar.

And she *wasn't* reading anything into Zahid's interference, she told herself fiercely. She hadn't even considered that a man like him might be interested in 'playing' with someone like her. He was simply looking out for her, that was all—the way he always had done in the past.

'He what, Francesca?' prompted Zahid.

'He made me realise that I needed to take a good look at my life,' she said.

And hadn't she decided that her doomed affair with Simon ought to have some lasting effect other than making her feel like a fool and a failure? That it was time to stop letting things *happen* to her and to have the courage to reach out to try to grasp them for herself. Wasn't that the reason why she'd plucked up the courage to come here today—even though her heart had been skittering with nerves from the moment she'd left home?

'I realised that I'd worked myself into a bit of a dead-end,' she continued slowly. 'That my life was going nowhere.'

Curiously, Zahid looked at her, remembering the little girl in her father's laboratory who had been given her own space on the bench, with her own test tubes and an oversized white coat to wear. 'I thought you wanted to be a scientist, like your father,' he said slowly.

Frankie shook her head. 'I was never as talented as he was. But I loved it—that's why I used to hang around the lab so much when I was young. And when he got ill my school work suffered—not that I'd ever particularly been happy at school.' She'd been too easy a target for the cruel-tongued girls who loved to mock the odd-looking child whose flighty mother had brought such shame on the family.

'And then there was the house and the garden to look after,' she added. Life had caught hold of her like a piece of flotsam and she'd allowed herself to drift around until her father had died and she'd found the job with Simon.

She knew that now she had some experience she might be able to get a job in one of the rival estate agencies—but she didn't want one. Not any more. She didn't want to stay in the same small town, but she didn't want to move just for the sake of it. She didn't really know *what* she wanted—just that she wanted something different. Something exciting. Something to make her forget the humiliation of her broken engagement. She looked up into Zahid's narrowed and watchful black eyes.

'I can type and I can file,' she finished. 'I can deal with people and I can problem solve. And I can cook, of course.'

It was an unusual combination, he mused as he

studied her. A woman with a neglected scientific talent who was also a great cook. Though when he stopped to think about it—wasn't cooking all about chemistry?

And speaking of chemistry…what about the other kind? The kind which was making him notice the pinpointing of her nipples which were thrusting against the navy dress and turning an otherwise commonplace outfit into something which was demanding to be peeled off. He looked into her wide-spaced blue eyes and felt the sizzle of danger in the air.

'I already have people to cook and to file for me,' he said evenly.

'I realise that.'

'Then what exactly are you asking me for, Francesca?'

She bit her lip, some of her nerve deserting her—until she remembered that if she wanted to take control of her own life, then wasn't this the first step? She had to reach out and ask—not be deterred by the first obstacle which was put in her way. 'I have no idea, Zahid. You were the one who made the offer that you could find me a job, remember? Although perhaps you didn't mean it at the time.'

There was a moment's silence before Zahid walked over to a book which lay open on the walnut writing desk, giving himself time to think. Was she trying to insult him by implying that he had made an empty offer—or was she simply calling his bluff?

He closed the book and looked up, still not saying anything. He could see anxiety vying with bravado on her face. Such a pale face, he thought and in amid his own warring feelings he felt a twist of concern; of the old, familiar protectiveness. Didn't she deserve a break? A chance to get away from the scurrilous Simon and the bad memories he'd helped create?

But it wasn't that easy.

He'd recognised that offering Francesca such an opportunity had been a mistake, for many reasons. It was unheard of in his country for a woman to work closely for a member of the ruling family. Perhaps he could have swung it if he'd been remaining in England for a while, but he wasn't. He was due to go home to Khayarzah within the next few days, and how could he possibly take her with him—a single Englishwoman living within the strict confines of palace life?

But Zahid also recognised that these reservations were all easily overcome and that the main stumbling block was the fact that he had begun to *desire* her with a hunger which at times had overwhelmed him. *And he couldn't afford to do that.*

Since that last meeting, hadn't he been thinking about her in a way which was most uncharacteristic? He enjoyed women and they enjoyed him—but he didn't get hung up about them. Not ever. Sometimes not even when he was thrusting into them and watching dispassionately as they orgasmed around him and squealed their joy. One of his own perceived strengths was emotional detachment and it had always served him well.

Yet for days now he'd been remembering Francesca's firm body and her soft, unpainted lips. The way she made him smile when he least expected it. Those deep blue eyes, which had stared at him from the confusion of his unusually restless and troubled dreams. Even when his sometime Russian lover Katya had arrived the other night—wearing nothing but a fur coat and a pair of tiny, crotchless panties—he had sent her away without making love to her.

Why the hell had he done that?

Wouldn't the best thing of all be for him to send Francesca away, too?

Because Zahid recognised that something had changed between them—and changed for ever. He no longer saw her as simply Francesca, his innocent childhood friend. He saw her now as a woman—a sexy and experienced woman who had just emerged from a bruising experience. And wasn't that dangerous?

Wouldn't she be feeling very natural frustration now that her relationship with Simon had ended? Wasn't there a danger that close confinement might prove too much of a temptation for them both?

He saw her reach out to touch the petals of a spray of orchids with light, tentative fingers and he was just imagining how delicate her touch might be on his aching skin when the telephone rang.

The sound ruptured his reverie. 'Answer it,' he said abruptly.

'But—'

'I said, answer it.'

Frankie's heart was thudding as she walked over towards the bureau and picked up the phone. Should she announce that it was the sheikh's phone? Probably not. It could so easily be the press. 'Hello?'

A woman's sultry and faintly disgruntled voice came down the line. 'Who the hell are you?'

Frankie's fingers tightened around the receiver; she felt fired up by some unknown instinct which had the little hairs on the back of her neck prickling. She wanted to say, "Who the hell are *you*?", but something stopped her and that something was Zahid watching her very closely. 'May I help you?' she questioned politely.

'Sure you can. I want to speak to Zahid.'

There was the briefest of pauses before Frankie spoke. 'I'm afraid that the sheikh is unavailable at the moment.' From the other side of the room, she saw Zahid raise his eyebrows in silent question. 'But if you'd like to give me your name and number, I'll make sure he gets it.'

'My name is Katya,' snapped the voice. 'And he already has my number—tell him to damned well use it!'

The connection was broken abruptly and Frankie replaced the phone, looking up to find Zahid's now inscrutable expression fixed on her. Her heart was thudding fiercely and she wondered who the woman with the sultry voice was.

'Who was it?' he demanded.

'Katya.'

His eyes narrowed. 'You didn't bother checking whether I wanted to speak to her?'

Awkwardly, Frankie wriggled her shoulders. Had she overstepped the mark and allowed her feelings of undeniable jealousy to influence her reaction?

'She sounded slightly…angry,' she explained, in a sudden rush. 'And I thought that the call might be of a personal nature, which you probably wouldn't care to take in front of me. Alternatively, if I'd asked you whether you wished to take the call and you'd declined—then that would have been embarrassing for all three of us. I made a judgement, Zahid—which is presumably the reason you asked me to answer your phone.' Tentatively, she chewed on her lip as he continued to stare at her in that expressionless way. 'Was it the wrong one?'

There was a pause while he regarded her thoughtfully. A bold judgement, he thought as he met the question in her deep blue eyes. And a brave one, too. He saw the sudden flush of colour which had flared into her pale cheeks. Had she guessed that Katya was a lover? An *ex*-lover, he reminded himself as he shook his head.

'No, it was not the wrong one—it was exactly right. I wanted to see whether you could think on your feet and it seems that you can,' he said softly. 'It's a pity you couldn't have been that insightful when you fell into bed with that creep Simon.'

For a moment, Frankie felt close to giving him a confessional, wondering if she should enlighten him about the laughably true nature of her relationship with Simon. But prospective employees didn't suddenly start talking about their sex lives, did they? 'It's easy to be insightful when you're acting for somebody else.'

'Well, you've got yourself a job.'

'I have?'

'Don't look so shocked.' He gave a short laugh because it seemed that she hadn't lost her ability to twist him around her little finger, after all. 'It was pretty much on the cards all along.'

'And what sort…what sort of job will it be?'

There was a brief silence as he allowed the long-standing glimmerings of an idea to float to the surface of his mind. 'My father once kept a diary,' he said slowly. 'Did I ever tell you that?'

She shook her head. 'No.'

'Writing it became a kind of refuge for him,' he continued. 'Particularly in the troubled years during the wars and then when my mother became ill. And it suddenly occurred to me that you might be just the person to type them up for me.'

'But I can't speak your language,' she objected.

'He wrote them in English.' He met her uncomprehending expression and shrugged. 'It ensured their privacy—since most of my people don't speak the language. I've been meaning to make them into a formal record for some time—the difficulty was in finding someone I could trust to do it.' His black eyes gleamed. 'And you, my dear Francesca, will be absolutely perfect for the task.'

Frankie blushed with pleasure—because praise from Zahid felt like the very best sort of praise.

'Does that sort of role appeal to you?' he questioned.

She nodded, trying not to be affected by the silken texture of his voice, but it wasn't easy. 'I'd like that very much.' She hesitated. 'You know, you haven't even mentioned why you're here—in England.'

He thought back to the working breakfast he'd had that morning with England's leading horse-racing experts—and the similar meetings which had taken place in every major city in Europe. With an effort, he switched his attention away from the soft rose-pink of her cheeks and the sapphire gleam of her eyes.

'I've been promoting the new horse-racing track and stadium we've almost completed in Khayarzah,' he said. 'One which will put us firmly on the international equestrian circuit. But this particular trip has also been personal.' He walked over to the window and stared at a rusty barge which was chugging its way down the heavy grey waters of the Thames. He wouldn't have discussed such a matter with anyone else, but his inherent trust in Francesca made him more candid than was usual. And didn't it come as a kind of liberation—to be able to speak his mind for once? 'I needed to meet with my brother,' he said as he turned back to face her. 'To see if he's really been behaving as badly as the media suggest.'

Frankie saw the sudden tension which had tightened his face and she wrinkled her nose in question.

She'd only met his brother Tariq on a few occasions—and one of those had been at her father's funeral, when she'd been too fogged down in grief to be able to think straight.

Like Zahid, Tariq had enjoyed a mixed and fairly liberal upbringing—some of it spent far away from his homeland. But the destinies of two princes could be so radically different...

When Zahid had become King, his life had changed immeasurably—while Tariq was still able to behave pretty much as he always had done. Frankie knew that the younger prince was known for being outrageously gorgeous and had been dubbed 'The Playboy Sheikh' by the more extravagant sections of the western press.

'Why, what has he done?' she questioned.

'That's just the point. He hasn't done nearly enough.' Zahid gave a little click of irritation. 'Well, that's not entirely true, since Tariq possesses the uncanny ability to produce excellent results with the minimum amount of work. He just needs a little reminding from time to time that he is a royal prince with an obligation to his country—and not simply an habitué of the gambling tables and an object of slavish female desire. But let us not talk about that now. You will fly with me to Khayarzah at the end of the week—do you have a passport?'

She nodded, aware how parochial his question made her sound. 'Of course.'

'And we need to get you settled. In fact, we'd better find you a room here.'

Taken aback, Frankie blinked at him. 'You mean I'm going to be staying *here*, at the Granchester?'

Something in the innocent way she framed the question sparked an unwanted hunger deep inside him—so that for a moment Zahid forgot that she was almost like one of the family. Forgot that his groin was not supposed to tighten and throb as he looked at her. Because when her pink and unpainted lips opened like that, he suddenly found he could think of a much better use for them than talking…

Unwanted lust made him tease her—trying to make his arousal go away but wondering idly whether she would respond. *And how would you react if she did? Would you take her in your arms and taste her? Treat you both to a sweet interlude of mutually satisfying sex?*

'Of course you're going to be staying here,' he murmured, shifting his position slightly, which did precisely nothing to relieve the deep ache at his groin. 'You'll need to make a few preparations before we fly to Khayarzah. You'll need a visa. Security clearance—that kind of thing—and it will all have to be done in London. You don't have a problem with that, do you?'

It took a moment for Frankie to answer because her body was responding crazily to the way he was looking at her. She could feel the prickle of her breasts and a strange pooling of heat at the pit of her stomach so that she felt all light-headed, and vulnerable. Was this something he did to all women—made them feel all kinds of stuff they weren't supposed to be feeling—leaving them aching and unsettled and wanting more?

But Frankie was determined to appear professional. He had seen her being made a fool of by her ex-fiancé—and her pride was hurting because of that. She must show him that she could be strong—that she wasn't some vulnerable little girl who jumped every time somebody made a loud bang.

'No, not a problem at all,' she said calmly. 'I'm very adaptable.'

'Good. Then come and meet the rest of my staff. I'll introduce you to my bodyguards and they'll explain a few simple guidelines to you.' He glanced down at her rain-spattered legs and the shoes which didn't quite match the plain blue dress. 'And we'd better organise some clothes for you. You'll need something appropriate to wear—especially in Khayarzah, where it's very hot but women cover their legs and their arms at all times. Something which befits a staff member to the sheikh.'

Frankie looked down at the dress she'd bought

specially for this meeting—wondering if he had any idea of all the angst which had gone into choosing the neat garment. 'You mean there's something wrong with what I'm wearing?'

Did he protect her from the truth, or did he give it to her straight? Zahid's mouth hardened. Hadn't she already been lied to enough by one man? And she would never learn about life's harsh realities unless somebody taught her. He looked her straight in the eye. 'There's nothing fundamentally *wrong* with it, Francesca—other than that it's cheap.' He gave her a regretful shrug as he reached out to pick up the phone. 'And I'm afraid I don't do cheap.'

CHAPTER SIX

PLONKING herself down on the bed, Frankie kicked the shoes from her aching feet and fell back against the snowy bank of pillows. It had been a long day. Even longer than yesterday, when she'd travelled back down to Surrey, packed some essentials and locked up the house—ready to embrace her new role as a member of Zahid's staff. Already, her world seemed to have altered out of all recognition. She'd been given a luxurious room in one of London's smartest hotels, a list of all the people who worked for the sheikh—as well as his busy schedule for the weeks ahead.

And today she had been sent off to see a stylist and to acquire the clothes which Zahid had told her were essential for her working trip to his homeland.

She hadn't realised that shopping could be so

exhausting—but then she didn't usually buy an entire wardrobe at one fell swoop. The swish store was situated in a side street, not far from the Khayarzah Embassy, and Frankie was put in the hands of an elegant woman who seemed to know exactly the kind of clothes she needed for her forthcoming trip.

The shopping expedition had been so intensive that she'd missed lunch and by the time she got back to the hotel she was too exhausted to bother with room service. So she ate the chocolate which had been left lying on her pillow and lay down on the bed just to rest her eyes.

She must have dozed off because before she knew it she was startled out of some bizarre and fitful dream about telephones by an urgent knocking on the door. Reluctantly, Frankie got up off the feathery mattress and padded across the room to answer it. Still yawning, she pulled open the door to find Zahid standing there with a look of unmistakable irritation on his face.

'I've been calling and calling you—didn't you hear me?'

Still dozy from an unfamiliar daytime nap, she raked her fingers through her tousled hair. 'No, of course I didn't—otherwise I'd have answered.' With difficulty, she stifled another yawn. 'Sorry—I must have fallen asleep.'

'Clearly.' Reluctantly, Zahid found his eyes drawn to her. Her cheeks were flushed and her lashes looked like ebony smudges making spiky shadows on her soft cheek. With her hair spilling down untidily over her shoulders, she looked as if she had just been ravished, he thought—with an unwelcome beat of awareness. But she was wearing an old pair of jeans and an oatmeal-coloured sweater he recognised and he frowned. 'I thought you'd been out shopping?'

'I have. I just got back.' She saw him looking askance at her jeans and shrugged as his gaze travelled over to the still open doors of her wardrobe, where the new clothes could be seen hanging in a neat line. 'They seem almost too nice to wear—does that sound stupid?'

'Yes.'

'Especially when I'm just mooching around the hotel room.'

'Well, stop mooching and start getting ready,' he said coolly. 'We're having dinner with my brother in just over an hour.'

'You're kidding?'

He sucked in a breath of irritation as he glanced at the rumpled bed directly behind her. 'No, Francesca, I am not. And just remember that I'm not paying you to lie around...' Now why had his mind focused on *that* particular verb? Dragging his gaze away from the ruffled duvet, he narrowed his eyes as he spotted a discarded chocolate wrapper lying on the carpet. 'Eating chocolate all day and napping! Be ready in an hour,' he ordered. 'One of my bodyguards will let you know when we're ready to go.'

He slammed the door shut behind him and for a moment Frankie stood staring at it in disbelief. Talk about leaping to the wrong conclusions! He'd made her sound like some decadent couch potato who loved stuffing her face with carbs—

when pretty much all she'd eaten all day had been that one, measly chocolate.

But she enjoyed soaking in a scented bath—and afterwards selecting something silken and suitable from her newly acquired wardrobe. The clothes she had been guided towards were fundamentally modest—there wasn't a low neck or a miniskirt in sight. Their beauty lay in the quality of the exquisite fabrics as they whispered delicately over her skin. As she slid on her own bra and knickers she thought that they seemed positively *dingy* in comparison to the quiet opulence of the green silk gown she'd chosen to wear.

One of Zahid's enigmatic-looking bodyguards rapped at the door at eight o'clock precisely, and Frankie stepped into the corridor to find Zahid just emerging from his own room. He was wearing a suit of pale grey, which served as a perfect foil for his bronzed and dark colouring. But he stopped dead when he saw her and stood completely still—as if someone had turned him to stone.

'Are you…ready?' she asked tentatively, wondering if she had committed some awful faux pas that she wasn't aware of. Was the dress too formal? Her shoes too high? Should she have worn her hair up instead of letting it tumble loosely down her back?

In answer to her stumbled question Zahid nodded—though he wasn't really listening to what she'd asked him. Because, against all the odds—she looked *beautiful*. More beautiful than any woman he had ever seen. Like some princess who had stepped from the pages of one of the old Khayarzah fables his nanny used to read to him as a child.

Her dark hair was glossy, her blue eyes wide and watchful—and the deep green of her dress emphasised the porcelain paleness of her face and soft curves of her body. What must it be like for her, he wondered, to have blossomed as she had blossomed—to have gone from tomboy to temptress in one seamless step? Was she aware of the power which now lay at her fingertips— the power possessed by every woman who could hold a man in her thrall?

Yet *Simon* had been the one to awaken her, he reminded himself grimly. He might have been a duplicitous and money-grubbing creep—but he was responsible for this new, sensual allure of hers. He had been the one who had…who had…

'Is this okay, Zahid?' Aware that his bright, hard gaze was still fixed on her, Frankie brushed her palms down over the silk skirt of her dress and gave him an anxious look. Why on earth was he scowling at her like that? 'The dress, I mean?'

'Are you searching for a compliment?' he queried, more acidly than he had intended—but he was having to quash a reaction to her that he had not intended and did not particularly want. The kind of reaction which would have usually culminated in him peeling her brand-new dress from her body and tossing it contemptuously to the floor, thus ensuring that they would be late for dinner. 'I'm sure you're perfectly aware that it's more than okay and that you look very… agreeable,' he finished.

Her smile was uncertain as she looped a big

cashmere wrap around her shoulders. *Agreeable?* Was that supposed to have been a compliment? She wasn't sure—not when he had managed to make it sound like some sort of growled *insult*.

Frankie felt nervous as they went downstairs to the car—a short journey which seemed to involve a lot of high-powered and pre-arranged choreography. Cocooned by a small phalanx of bodyguards, Zahid walked at speed through the lobby—seemingly oblivious to the curious eyes which were darted in his direction—with her tottering on high heels behind him.

A limousine was waiting outside the hotel—its door already open and engine purring—and as Frankie sat back against the squishy, soft leather seat she wondered how all this could have happened—and so quickly. Why, only last week she'd been showing a couple around a new-build and today she was being whisked through central London in a luxury limousine, with a brooding-looking sheikh sitting beside her.

She splayed her fingers out over her lap. He seemed *uncomfortably* close—so that the atmosphere seemed full of his own particular scent. A potent cocktail of raw male mixed with sweet sandalwood and the tang of lemons was now invading her senses. And somehow he was managing to imprint his powerful body onto her subconscious, even though she was pointedly looking out of the car window in an attempt to lessen the impact he was having on her. What on earth was the matter with her? Shouldn't she have been missing Simon—if only a little bit— instead of fantasising what it might be like if Zahid pulled her into his arms and began to kiss her?

'Where…where are we going?' she questioned breathlessly. 'And tell me a bit more about what Tariq is doing these days.'

Zahid watched with interest as she dug her nails into one silk-covered thigh. Much more of that and she would claw tiny holes into that new dress of hers, he thought. 'There's a private members' club next door to The Ivy—and we're meeting him there. He lives in England permanently now.'

'*Does* he? Doing what?'

'He runs the European arm of the family business—but he also has a very successful polo club in the south of England which he bought quite recently.'

Of course he does, thought Frankie as the car coasted past the shining shop lights which lightened the dark November night and drew to a halt in front of a discreet door. She knew that Tariq was a superb and talented polo player, so it followed that he would have a club of his own. The Al Hakam family never did anything by halves.

Inside the private members' club, masses of flowers stood in eye-catching arrangements and a glass lift zoomed them up to a large room which somehow managed to have an intimate feel to it. In one corner, a grand piano was being played softly by an aging crooner who smiled at them as they walked in—and on a nearby table, Frankie recognised a soap-star who was more famous for her chequered love-life than for her work as an actress.

They were ushered towards a small, private

dining room and when they arrived Tariq was already seated at the table. It was the first time that Frankie had ever seen the brothers together—and with their dramatically dark good looks, the family resemblance was startling. But the younger brother was wearing faded jeans and a silk shirt—his shadowed jaw resolutely unshaven—and he had an air of slightly disreputable charm, which was at odds with Zahid's rather more formal appearance.

He rose to his feet when he saw them approach and the two men embraced. And then as Tariq let his arms fall away he gave Frankie a smile which she suspected had made many women melt into a puddle at his feet.

'How unusual. It's not like you to bring a woman with you, Zahid,' he observed, his voice a honeyed murmur. 'So who is *this* little beauty?'

Zahid glared at his sibling. 'This is Francesca.'

'Francesca?' There was a pause as Tariq frowned and then his face suddenly cleared as he made the connection. 'Frankie? *Frankie?* I don't believe it! Is that really you?'

'Yes!' She smiled back as he gathered her in a bear hug and she realised that Zahid had said pretty much the same thing. Which begged the question of how much she had changed. Did she really look that different? She guessed she did. Yet it was funny how you could be altered so radically on the exterior—and yet inside you felt exactly the same...with all those same nagging doubts and insecurities. 'Yes, it's really me!'

'Wow! You look so *different*. Amazing! All pretty, and grown-up. Good heavens...' Tariq frowned. 'You and Zahid, I mean you aren't—'

'We aren't anything,' Zahid snapped, giving his brother another furious glare. 'Francesca is working for me now.'

'*Is* she now? That's quite a bold step.'

'But maybe it's about time. Such an appointment will show the western world that we do take women seriously. And it will pacify some of the more rebellious females back home in Khayarzah.'

Tariq laughed. 'There speaks my brother, the

King! How completely ruthless you can be, Zahid.'

'You think so? I prefer to describe myself as a realist.' Zahid shrugged. 'And why not capitalise on opportunity when it comes knocking?'

Frankie bit her lip as she heard herself described as an 'opportunity'.

'Wine, Frankie?' asked Tariq.

'I'd better not—'

'Nonsense. If Zahid wants to show the world he's tolerant and open to the ways of the west, then he should let his pretty guest have a glass of wine even if he doesn't much care for it himself.'

She rarely drank but Frankie suddenly found herself longing for a glass. So many emotional missiles had been hurled at her over the last few days and she still felt a little dazed by it all. Her whole pattern of living had crashed and she hadn't quite got used to the new, rebooted version. She knew that she should be feeling more pain about the end of her relationship with Simon—but the crazy thing was that she didn't. And that in turn made her feel guilty. She kept questioning her own judgment and every time she did it filled her with a feeling of failure. A drink might help relax her.

'Thank you,' she said, ignoring the narrow-eyed look which Zahid sent shooting in her direction. 'I think I will.'

The meal was a mixture of glamour and grit. Frankie was aware that she was in a high-octane atmosphere and being served some of the best food in the capital. But she felt strangely removed from it all—as if she was an outsider, looking in.

Maybe that wasn't so surprising. She was with two members of a royal family and they spent a lot of the evening speaking—and arguing—in their native tongue. Consequently, she found herself sipping at the rich red wine without really noticing and before she knew it she was halfway through a second glass. Her cheeks had begun to burn and Zahid was frowning at her across the table—and suddenly she found herself lost in the judgemental razoring of his gaze. Her tongue snaked out to encircle lips which had suddenly become bone-dry and she could have sworn she saw his eyes darken in response.

'Don't have anything more to drink, Francesca.'

She hadn't been intending to—at least, not until he clipped out that peremptory order. 'Why, are you *rationing* me now?' she questioned. 'This is only my second glass.'

Zahid felt irritated. It had been bad enough that his younger brother was stubbornly refusing to listen to reason and take his advice—without Francesca suddenly throwing her inhibitions to the wind. Why the hell had Tariq foisted that wine on her—and why had she let him?

'You're clearly not used to it. Come on,' he said abruptly, rising to his feet. 'It's time we were going.'

'But I haven't had any pudding!' she protested.

'Wasn't the chocolate you were eating earlier enough to satisfy your sweet cravings?' questioned Zahid acidly.

'But I only had one—and I missed lunch!'

Dark eyes looked positively *frozen* now. 'You

can order something from room service when we get back,' he snapped. 'And fascinating as this conversation is, I feel we must deprive my brother of any more of it.'

But Tariq was laughing. 'Oh, please don't let me stop you—I don't think I've ever heard you sounding quite so *domesticated*, Zahid.'

Frankie's feisty mood had evaporated by the time she retrieved her cashmere wrap from the cloakroom, and Tariq slid it round her shoulders with automatic courtesy. Why couldn't Zahid do a gentlemanly thing like that, she wondered wistfully—instead of glaring at her as if she had suddenly become radioactive? She stepped out into the cold night and the drop in temperature was so dramatic that she stumbled a little until Zahid caught her elbow and steadied her.

She could feel his fingers burning through the fine cashmere of her wrap and she saw his mouth grow taut, before he gently manoeuvred her into the limousine as it slid to a halt beside them.

He turned to his brother, his face tense and his voice low. 'Just remember what I said. You are now the brother of the sheikh—the heir. You shouldn't be associated with a woman like that, a woman who is…'

Frankie had been listening intently to their conversation but rather annoyingly he had said the last word in his native language—or rather, he hissed it out like a cornered snake she had once seen at the zoo.

'Who's Tariq going out with who you obviously don't approve of?' she questioned, after they'd said goodbye and the car was pulling away.

'Nobody,' he answered tersely.

'But I just heard you say—'

'Well, you shouldn't have done. You should have blocked the sound out. Don't you know what they say about eavesdroppers?'

'If I'm supposed to be working for you, and if you're supposed to trust me, then don't I need to know these things?'

'Not *now*, Francesca! You will know what I wish you to know and when I wish you to know it. But top of the list of my requirements is an assurance that you do *not* persist with a line in

questioning when your sheikh has expressly forbidden it. Do you understand?'

He had never spoken to her like that before.
Never. Not once had he ever pulled rank—and
Frankie shrank back against the seat of the car
as she realised that this was the price she must
pay for working for him. She was no longer to be
indulged and protected by him—but to be treated
as he would treat any other member of his staff.
And didn't a stupid and stubborn little part of her
suddenly long for some of the slightly indulgent
and caring attitude which he'd always shown to
her before? 'I think you've made yourself very
clear,' she said, in a small voice.

He turned towards her, his mood made sombre
by his younger brother's stubbornness—but
something in the crestfallen expression on her
face wiped the anger clean out of his head and
replaced it with something entirely different.

Her lips were trembling and her face was pale.
Framed by the soft cashmere of her wrap, the
dark green silk of her dress seemed to be strain-
ing against the weight of her luscious breasts.

And legs. He swallowed down the sudden hot surge of lust. What about her legs? When she crossed them like that, was she aware that the delicate silk moulded against the outline of her thighs and that her shapely ankles would drive any normal, hot-blooded man crazy with desire?

He wanted to kiss her.

He wanted to tear away the silk-satin to see those breasts for himself before tasting their rosy tips. He wanted to slide the dress still further up her legs and make her hot and sweet and wet for him.

He must be out of his mind!

Shifting his position further along the seat, Zahid stared at her with an expression which would have made his sage old advisors back in Khayarzah shiver with apprehension if they'd seen it. But his fury was directed at himself.

What the hell was he playing at?

'Cover your legs!' he bit out.

His furious words crashed in and shattered Frankie's pensive mood and she sat up and returned his angry stare, her eyes bewildered. Her *legs*? Why, there was hardly any of her legs on show—barely even a flash of ankle! Perhaps she *hadn't* been sitting in a way which was very ladylike, but even so—there was no need for him to shout. She leaned forward to tug at her skirt but that didn't seem to please him either.

'Is this the way you behave when you go out for dinner with a man?' he demanded. 'Quaffing wine by the glass and wriggling around in the back of a car with a dress which looks at least one size too small?'

'No! *No!* I told you—I hardly drink a thing. And the dress is a perfect fit! Don't be so old-fashioned, Zahid!'

'But I *am* old-fashioned!' he thundered, before the hypocrisy of his own words hit him. He wasn't *usually* old-fashioned when it came to women, was he? Usually, the more outrageous the outfit, the more he enjoyed it. He thought of Katya the other night, turning up in nothing but her glittery panties and a fur coat and his mouth thinned. He hadn't enjoyed *that* very much, had he?

'We are almost at the hotel,' he said in a cold voice. 'Do you think you can possibly manage to make it upstairs on your own, without stumbling?'

She'd never heard him sound quite so *frosty* before—or so angry—and Frankie puckered her lips together, afraid that she might top off the evening with something unforgivable—like bursting into tears. Had she had made another serious misjudgement, thinking that the answer to her problems had been to grab at this job? Had she really thought that working for Zahid might be some sort of *adventure*?

Well, she had been wrong. Now they seemed to do nothing but rub each other up the wrong way and she would tell him so. She would tell him that she had made a mistake and that she would be staying in England after all. But not tonight. She wanted tonight to end as soon as possible. She would inform him in the cold, clear light of day that it was probably better if she looked elsewhere for a job. 'Of course I can,' she answered flatly.

Their little convoy of cars drew to a halt and they travelled up in the lift together—an awkward little group which consisted of a stony-faced Zahid, a Frankie who was trying very hard not to let her lips wobble and two bodyguards who were built like bulldogs.

And when they reached their floor and Frankie had extracted her key-card, her fumbling fingers somehow prevented her from getting the door open and Zahid plucked it from her with a click of irritation.

For a moment their fingers brushed together and her eyes widened in startled recognition of the sudden warm thrill of that brief, physical contact. Irresistibly, their gazes locked and she saw the sudden darkening of his eyes. For one crazy second she observed the soft parting of his lips and the breath froze in her throat. *Was Zahid attracted to her—as she was to him?* Was he leaning forward as if he was about to *kiss* her?

But then the moment passed and he turned

away. Her heart was beating frantically as he swiped the key-card and this time the light went on.

'Ah, I'm getting the green light again,' he said sardonically, unable to resist the sensual taunt—but she made no response to it. And he found himself wondering what he would have done if she had taunted him right back…

Frankie set her face into a frozen little smile. Was he laughing at her? Making fun of her? Her heart gave a painful lurch but she kept her face completely expressionless. 'Goodnight, Zahid,' she said quietly. 'Thank you very much for dinner.'

Her dignified statement filled him with a sudden feeling of guilt and Zahid wasn't quite sure what had provoked it. Perplexed, he watched as she closed the door behind her and he was left standing outside Francesca's bedroom with a distinctly rare feeling of frustration.

CHAPTER SEVEN

ZAHID slept restlessly for much of the night. He was troubled by the stubbornness of his brother and the life he seemed to be leading. But he was troubled by something else, too—and that something was desire.

He opened his eyes. Nothing new there. Desire was as much a part of his life as eating. He had the healthy appetite of a man in his glorious prime and enjoyed sex as much as he enjoyed hunting, or riding—or seeing his beloved falcon soar up into the azure splendour of the Khayarzah skies.

But he had never made the connection between sex and *emotion* before—mainly because the latter did not figure greatly in his life. Early on, he had recognised that it was useful for a king to be emotionally detached. Maybe it was useful for *all* men to be so.

Emotion was messy—and so was depending on only one person—everyone knew that. Wasn't he grateful that his position as King meant that he would never be required to walk such a potentially explosive path?

Pushing back the sweat-damp sheets, he got out of bed and walked naked into the bathroom, where he stood beneath a cold shower. The icy jets of water lashed down onto his tense and overheated body to briefly offer some relief. But not for very long.

His erotic dreams of last night had disturbed him—and they disturbed him still—because this time they were not easily fixed. For once, the dreams had not been of some beauty he'd met at some function, whom he could summon at will and have writhing beneath him before the day was out. Someone with whom he could enjoy a sweet, no strings affair—before kissing them goodbye with a significant piece of jewellery to remember him by.

Because the face which had haunted him all night long had been that of Francesca.

Francesca O'Hara.

He groaned as he lathered soap over his hips, feeling the heavy throb of desire at his groin and praying that the ice-water would quickly dispel these useless fantasies. Because they *were* fantasy. She was *completely forbidden* to him—and he had to force himself to remember why.

He had known her all her life.

Her father had trusted him.

Most important of all, there was no future for her with him—because she was English and he was Khayarzahian. The destinies ordained for each of them were radically different—and she meant too much to him to ever want to hurt her. Because although Francesca O'Hara was an experienced woman of the world with one fiancé already behind her, he respected her too much to offer her nothing but a quick fling.

The thought of Simon robbing Francesca of her precious innocence was enough to kill Zahid's desire stone-dead and abruptly he turned off the shower, towelled himself dry and dressed.

His breakfast laid up on the table beside him, he'd just hit the 'send' button on an email when there was a rap at the door—quickly followed by a soft English voice.

'Zahid?'

'Come in.'

He looked up as the door opened slowly and Francesca stood there, her expression more than a little anxious, wearing some sort of muted grey dress which seemed to have leached all the colour from her face.

'Zahid—'

'You'd better come in and shut the door behind you,' he commanded softly.

She did as he asked, drawing in a deep breath. 'I need to talk to you.'

'Talk away. But at least let's do it in some degree of comfort.' He gestured towards the table which was laid with breakfast, in an alcoved window overlooking the city. 'Have you had breakfast?'

'No. I'm not…very hungry.'

'Francesca.' He gave a slightly impatient sigh as he rose to his feet and walked over to her, taking her firmly by the elbow and steering her towards the table. But he felt the unmistakable tension in her body when he touched her and the answering clamour of his own senses in response. 'On a current showing, you aren't impressing me with your daily diet. All this skipping meals simply will not do. Coffee?'

She wanted to tell him that she was leaving but now he was propelling her into a chair and pouring her a cup of inky-dark coffee and somehow had persuaded her to take a warm croissant from the linen cradle of the bread basket.

Under his fierce gaze, she tore a buttery strip from the pastry and held it in her fingers. 'Zahid, about last night—'

'Yes, I've been meaning to speak to you about last night.'

'You have?''

'Mmm.' He sipped at his coffee and looked at

her over the rim of the cup. 'But I'll hear what you have to say first.'

She thought that was a little unfair, but she was hardly in a position to say so. And it was hard to put anything into words when he was sitting right opposite her like that—managing to appear both relaxed and yet supremely powerful. With his fine silk shirt unbuttoned at the neck and his black hair still glittering from the shower, Frankie could have sat looking at him all day. But wasn't that precisely *why* she needed to do the decent thing and hand her notice in, before her stupid desire for him got out of hand?

'It seemed a good idea at the time to accept your offer,' she began. 'But clearly this isn't going to work. Or rather, *I'm* not going to work— at least, not for you. I can't come to Khayarzah, Zahid. I thought I could, but I can't. I'm sorry.'

'What a jumble of words!' He reached for a glass of juice. 'Why not?'

'Because you don't *treat* me fairly!' she objected.

'I don't?' he questioned coolly. 'I fail to see

how when I have just bought you an entire new wardrobe and will be paying you a very handsome salary to type up my father's diary.'

'That's not what I meant, and you know it.'

'Really?' He registered her spiky challenge with surprise. 'Then just what *do* you mean?'

She let the untouched piece of croissant flutter onto the plate. 'All that stuff last night about what I was wearing and the way I was sitting—and how I'd had too much to drink, when we both know I hadn't. That was all because you've known me all my life and still treat me like a child!'

'On the contrary,' Zahid said, sitting back in his chair and regarding her with unsettling scrutiny. 'On reflection, the reason I said all those things was because you *aren't* a child any more.'

Now it was her turn to look to him for clarification. Her brow creased in a puzzled frown. 'I don't understand.'

'I think you probably do—if you stop for a minute to think about it. You see, I'm used to thinking of you as a friend—my only real female friend, as it happens.'

The simple accolade affected her deeply and for a moment Frankie was filled with a fear that he was about to snatch it away from her. And suddenly she realised that no job in the world was worth *that*. 'Please don't make it sound as if it's all in the past!' she cried, before she had time to think about the wisdom of her words or that they had poured out so emotionally.

'I have no intention of making it something in the past,' he said, his voice gentling by a fraction. 'It's just that you have grown up into a beautiful and very desirable young woman—and I'm finding it difficult to know how to react to you.'

It was such a stark and honest admission that it took Frankie completely by surprise. She looked at him in disbelief until she found herself blushing and then glanced down at her plate, terrified about what he might read into her embarrassment. Did he have any idea that she had entertained stupid fantasies about him since the year dot?

For a full minute there was silence and when the tension in the air had grown to such a point that she couldn't take it any more, Frankie risked glancing up into his eyes once more.

'I don't know what to say,' she whispered.

And for once in his life, neither did Zahid.

Looking at the morning light as it fell on the dark gleam of her hair, he knew what he *should* say. He should tell her he agreed with her—that it was an impossible situation which he hadn't really thought through. That he hadn't expected desire to rear its powerful head—and maybe it was best if she *did* go. Yet to Zahid that smacked of failure, and he didn't *do* failure—not in any sphere of his life.

Now his gaze skated over the swell of her breasts, which seemed to transform the demure grey dress into a garment of shocking provocation. Wouldn't it be a formidable and life-affirming challenge to resist the temptation she represented? Like the times when he and his brother had travelled into the arid centre of the desert and denied themselves the soft comforts of palace life. Such deprivation had been imposed on them by their elders as a deliberate means of making them strong and tough. Wouldn't this simply be a variation on the same kind of denial?

'I am loath to let you go,' he admitted slowly. 'And the reasons for giving you the job haven't changed.'

'No.'

'But...' He hesitated. Didn't they know each other well enough to dispense with coy hints and get straight to the truth? He gave a rueful shrug of his shoulders. 'We're worried because something has changed and we've discovered that we are sexually attracted to each other.'

At this, she blushed. How *anatomical* he made it sound. 'Zahid!'

'Oh, come on, Francesca—don't play the outraged innocent.' His eyes gleamed. 'It's what we've both been thinking—or are you going to deny this rather inconvenient desire which has flared up between us?'

His black eyes were lasering into her and beneath their intensity she felt positively weak.

Inconvenient? Was that how he saw it? She shook her head, because surely she could be honest, too. 'No, I'm not going to deny it.'

'The trouble is that you're no longer the innocent little girl I remember,' he observed. 'You're a beautiful and experienced young woman who's just come out of a bruising bust-up.'

Experienced? He thought she was *experienced?* Frankie gave a weak smile in response. Well, of course he did. Why wouldn't he? Most modern engaged women were having fantastic sex with the man they were going to marry. The fact that she and Simon hadn't progressed much beyond 'first base' she'd put down to some pathetic idea that he was a gentleman—never realising that it was because he was enjoying an illicit passion with somebody else. Should she tell Zahid that? Should she come right out and say it?

Zahid, I'm still a virgin.

Wouldn't that make her look like a complete loser?

Of course it would.

He leaned back in his chair, watching the play

of emotions which shadowed her face. 'In fact, if it were anyone other than you, I'd be pulling you into my arms and kissing you right now and then dragging you off to the nearest bed before making love to you. But for all kinds of reasons, we both know that isn't going to happen,' he added, with a careless air which his protesting body didn't quite endorse. 'So you see, I completely understand why you don't want to come to Khayarzah. The question is whether or not you would be a fool not to do so?'

His words fell between them like a challenge— and Frankie suddenly felt as if he'd tied her up in verbal knots. Hadn't *she* been the one who had told him that she didn't think the job was such a good idea, after all? And wasn't *he* the one who had somehow managed to turn it around to make her want to reconsider her opinion?

Yet there was enough substance behind his question to *make* her reconsider. Because the truth of it was that it had been a long-time dream of hers to see the land which her father had helped mould with his discovery of its oil. A land which he had visited on many occasions and had enthused about with most uncharacteristic passion.

Frankie had always longed to see for herself the fabulous palace at Mangalsutra, the country's capital—with its beautiful, scented gardens which he had talked about so often. And hadn't she longed to eat some more of those crystallised walnuts she'd once tasted—bought from the colourful and bustling market which was held in the main square of the city?

'I've always wanted to go there,' she said truthfully, her eyes shining as she remembered the stories she'd grown up with. 'My father used to tell me all about the place. He said that in springtime, fields of poppies sprang up overnight— turning the landscape into a scarlet haze. That at night-time the moon was so big that you felt you could almost reach out and lasso it from the sky. And that leopards lived in the high mountains in the east—and sometimes a very lucky traveller might be able to spot one.'

'Well, then.' Zahid listened to the faraway

note in her voice—and found himself ridiculously touched by her knowledge and obvious love of his country. So many people dismissed the east as just a prolific provider of oil—as if Khayarzah consisted of nothing but refineries and gilded palaces! The only thing she had got wrong was the leopard—for he'd never known anyone who had seen the elusive creatures which were reputed to live on the eastern heights. But he had no intention of telling her that. Why destroy someone's dreams unless you had to?

He glittered her a cool smile. 'In that case, it seems to be that your destiny intends you to come to my country and see it for yourself.'

It was what she'd always wanted—but the tug in her heart alerted her to an unfamiliar kind of danger. And something in Zahid's now shuttered expression made a feeling of apprehension whisper over Frankie's skin.

CHAPTER EIGHT

HE DIDN'T look so urbane now.

'What's the matter, Francesca?' questioned Zahid softly.

The matter? Frankie stared at him. Did he mean apart from the fact that her heart was racing so fast that she felt dizzy? Or that her knees felt so weak, she was glad she was sitting down? With an effort she quashed the pervasive sense of desire which had hit her the moment he'd emerged from the concealed section situated at the back of his private jet. Because Frankie had never seen Zahid looking like *this* before.

Just before the Gulfstream jet had landed—descending like a silver bird from the darkening blue of the desert sky—he had disappeared to change. The very act of dressing and undressing on the aircraft had seemed an unbearably intimate act and Frankie was ill prepared for the sight which greeted her on his return. Because the sleek and sophisticated royal with whom she'd breakfasted in his penthouse suite seemed to be nothing but a distant memory.

Gone was the urbane image of the man he had been in London—the exquisitely cut Italian suit now replaced by robes of flowing white. She'd seen pictures of him in traditional dress before—but nothing on earth could have prepared her for the impact of seeing the real-life version.

The delicate fabric hinted at the hard body beneath and the blanched colour threw his burnished skin into stark relief. Jet-dark hair was covered by a white headdress held in place by a dark and intricately knotted circlet of scarlet.

Frankie couldn't tear her eyes away from him. Yes, he was a king—but somehow that seemed irrelevant in the light of his blatant masculinity. He looked almost...*primitive*, she thought as she swallowed down the sudden dryness in her mouth. *Elemental.* As if he had appeared from some bygone age where men were unashamedly men, and women were…

'Nervous?' he questioned drily.

'Not at all,' she lied.

'Then why are you wringing your hands so tightly together? *Relax*.'

Frankie looked down to see that her knuckles were as white as if she'd been on a roller-coaster ride. Because hadn't concerns plagued her during the flight from London? Perfectly legitimate concerns which made her question the wisdom of agreeing to accompany Zahid to Khayarzah.

She would be on *his* territory—and subject to *his* whim. In close contact with a man she desired. He had assured her that he wasn't going to seduce an old family friend—and had said it with a steely resolve that she didn't doubt for one minute. Yet the irony was that his words had left her with a dull and aching feeling of disappointment—even though she knew they made perfect sense.

As the plane came to a halt Frankie unclipped her seat belt. 'I wonder how my appearance is going to go down?' she questioned tentatively. 'Whether your people will approve?'

'I have given up trying to please everyone,' Zahid said in a suddenly harsh tone as he remembered his early days on the throne, and how he had not known whom he could trust. The previous sheikh had been very traditional and Zahid found that most of those old advisors were just as resistant to modernising the country as his uncle had been. 'I must just be true to myself and let myself be judged by my actions.' He stood up and gestured for her to follow him. 'But I am not anticipating many problems when it comes to your appearance—for let's not forget that you have a famous surname.'

'I'm not famous, Zahid,' she protested.

'No. But your father is. His name is taught in our schools as the man who discovered our rich resources. He's a little bit of a national hero—surely you realised that?' He saw the pleasure in her eyes, and a brief smile touched the edges of his lips. 'There will be a delegation waiting to meet me, but you'll soon get used to that. So do as I told you on the plane. Just keep your eyes averted—and walk a few paces behind me.'

She smoothed down the silk tunic top, with its matching narrow trousers. 'And my outfit…is it okay?' she questioned.

Reluctantly, Zahid studied her, allowing his eyes to linger on her youthful form. Cool, practical and decent, her clothes met all the necessary criteria which the country's strict dress-code required. Yet in spite of that they managed to make her look incredibly *sexy*—something he hadn't really been expecting. Was that because it hinted at the firm flesh which lay beneath—or because he knew he could never have her in the way he wanted?

Feeling the unwilling heat of desire begin to build, he turned away. 'It's fine,' he said abruptly as the aircraft steps were lowered. 'Now let's go.'

She followed him out into the cooling air of the Khayarzah evening, to see a row of officials waiting to greet their king. And it seemed that their initial looks of wariness were softened when she was introduced to them and the

'O'Hara' connection was made. Through the butterfly build-up of nerves, Frankie suddenly felt an overwhelming sense of pride in her father and what he had done for this country.

They journeyed to the palace in a sleek limousine and through the smoked glass of their car window she could see tall palms, their fronds dramatically etched against the perfect blue of the sky. The road was long and straight and smoother than any English road she'd encountered. Behind them she could hear the muffled roar of the outriders—and beside her sat Zahid, his powerful body swathed in white silk, incongruously speaking into a mobile phone in his native tongue.

They skirted the main city of Mangalsutra—with its winding streets and jumble of rooftops—until they reached the gates of the palace itself. The immense white marble building rose up before her, fronted by a long, rectangular space of water fringed by palm trees. Turrets and domes and shadowed arches were contrasted against the darkening sky in which she could already see the faint twinkle of stars. Slowly Frankie expelled the breath she had been holding and Zahid must have heard her because he shot her a glance.

'Beautiful, isn't it?'

'It's exquisite,' she answered simply.

And so was she, he thought achingly. Against all the odds—so was she. With those blue eyes widening in wonder and the pert thrust of her breasts filling him with dark and erotic impulses. Would it be so bad if, after a cursory but necessary introduction to key members of his staff, he took her off to his private quarters, stripped the concealing silk garments from her body and laid her bare? If he opened thighs which would inevitably be milky-pale as he thrust hungrily between them?

Angrily, he crossed one leg over another. Had he forgotten where he was? *Who* he was? More importantly, who *she* was?

'Come and meet my staff,' he said unsteadily.

Frankie was taken to meet another line of robed servants, but her senses were too full of all these new experiences to be able to remember many of their exotic-sounding names. And she was preoccupied with watching Zahid—for he was no longer just the long-standing family friend who had always been kind to her, but the leader of a desert kingdom. He was in charge, she realised—and he radiated an impressive kind of power.

Swallowed up by advisors and aides, she watched as solemn-looking men bowed and began briefing him in his native tongue. Someone handed him a sheaf of papers and then a phone began to ring and was passed to him. He seemed to have forgotten that she was there—for he barely raised his dark head as she left the gilded chamber.

A young girl of about seventeen called Fayruz had been assigned to look after her, and as Frankie was led along a marbled corridor lined with blue and gold mosaic she wondered how on earth she was going to be able to communicate with her. But to her surprise, it transpired that Fayruz spoke good—if slightly tentative—English.

'I learn it at school,' she said shyly, in response

to Frankie's question. 'It is my best subject—
which is why I have been brought in to assist
you while you are here.'

'You're at school still?'

'Oh, yes,' Fayruz offered shyly.

'And then what—university, I suppose?'

There was a pause. 'In my country, women are
not encouraged to go to university.'

Frankie frowned. 'You're kidding?'

Fayruz shook her head. 'It's thought women
make better mothers than scholars.' She gave a
small sigh and then shrugged her shoulders. 'I
will unpack for you now.'

'No, honestly—I can do that for myself,' said
Frankie, shaking her head in slight disbelief.
Women *not encouraged to go to university*? This
was much worse than she had imagined.

'Then let me draw a bath for you,' said Fayruz
eagerly. 'Please. You must be hot after your long
journey and the Sheikh will be displeased if I do
not show you Khayarzahian hospitality.'

Frankie nodded, recognising that she must
learn to adapt to a different way of living, to

graciously accept a slower pace and help when it was offered. And wouldn't it be good to freshen up and relax before dinner? 'Thank you,' she said quietly. 'That would be lovely.'

Lovely turned out to be something of an understatement—because when Fayruz called to say that the bath was ready, Frankie could hardly believe her eyes. A wide, square bath—big as a child's swimming pool—was filled with warm, rose-scented water on which floated fresh petals.

After the servant had gone, Frankie stripped off her clothes and slowly submerged herself in its scented depths, the silky water lapping over her. This was heaven. Bliss. She closed her eyes. The closest she'd ever come to pure indulgence. Lulled by the warm water and the total silence, she relaxed for a while before reluctantly climbing out of the cooling water to get ready for dinner.

Skimming her fingers over the row of silk outfits which now hung in the wardrobe, she picked a long dress of pure white. People often wore white in desert countries, didn't they? And Zahid had been robed in white earlier…

She'd just finished dressing when Fayruz tapped at the door and led her through a maze of intricate corridors to what was described as the 'small' dining room—but this proved to be yet another understatement. It was bigger than any dining room she'd ever seen and decorated lavishly in gold and lapis lazuli. Intricately tooled hanging lamps filled the room with a soft radiance and the scent of cinnamon and sandalwood wafted through the air. The table itself was low and, instead of chairs, there were brocade cushions heaped around it.

At that moment, Zahid swept into the room—a small, accompanying retinue of stern-faced men walking close behind him. Across the exotic room, their eyes met, and Frankie felt a sizzle of awareness warming her skin, beneath the silk gown.

'Hello, Zahid,' she said softly.

Lulled by the soft familiarity of her voice, Zahid slowly let his gaze travel over her. She

was wearing white—pure and virginal white—
and he felt his body clench with instinctive jealousy. Did she not realise the bitter irony of her
choice—she who no longer had the right to wear
the traditional hue of innocence? A black tide
of rage rose up in him as he remembered that
it had been the rogue Simon who had taken her
virginity.

He could see his advisors standing, waiting for
his command. He had intended to invite them
to stay—for their English was certainly good
enough. And it might dilute Frankie's undeniable
appeal if he was faced with the subtle censor-
ing of his aides. Yet now, on impulse he found
himself raising his hand to dismiss them and
they filed obediently from the room. Settling
himself on a pile of cushions so that his groin
was shielded by a thick swathe of his robes, he
indicated that she too should sit.

'Your room meets with your approval?' he
questioned.

Frankie sank down onto soft brocade. 'How
could it not? It's amazing.'

'And you are hungry, I hope?'

She couldn't possibly tell him that her interest in food had been eclipsed by the man sitting opposite her. With an effort, she tore her eyes away from the shockingly sensual outline of his mouth and glanced around the room with the rapt interest of a tourist. 'I'm looking forward to tasting some of your fabled Khayarzahian cuisine,' she answered politely.

Zahid narrowed his eyes. This was not the Francesca he knew, the one whose sharp wit he had always secretly admired. Why, she sounded like one of the many visiting ambassadors who regularly mouthed their platitudes!

'Then let us begin,' he said, nodding to the silent servants who were standing unobtrusively at the sides of the room and who then began to bring dishes of food in.

Frankie could only pick at the gleaming rice studded with pistachios and the dried fruits and soft cheeses—though she enjoyed the slightly fizzy date juice which Zahid called *Nadirah*. And all the time she tried to keep her eyes fixed on the plate in front of her, not daring to raise her face to his—fearful of what he might read in her eyes.

'You seem very…nervous tonight,' he observed softly. 'Or is there some special reason why you won't look at me?'

Reluctantly, she lifted her head to find his ebony stare burning into her like dark fire. She wondered how he would react if she told him the truth—that she longed for him to take her in his arms. To kiss her and never stop kissing her. All the things he'd told her weren't going to happen were all the things she *wanted* to happen. She forced her lips into the upward curve of a smile. Maybe a variation on the truth would suffice. 'I can't quite get used to seeing you here, being a king.'

Zahid nodded. Hadn't it taken time for *him* to get used to wearing the crown—to being the ruler of all he surveyed and the inevitable intoxication which came with it? Yet power came at a price, too—particularly when it came out of the blue.

When the plane carrying his uncle the king and

his only son had crashed during a storm, Zahid had been crowned the new king—a role he had never expected, nor particularly wanted. But it was a role he was determined to fulfil to the best of his ability, even though many had looked on him suspiciously. He was still working hard to earn the faith of the key palace advisors— and push forward his agenda to modernise the country. But it would take time to get consensus and to earn the trust of the government and the people of Khayarzah. But that kind of trust had *always* existed between him and Francesca— and he didn't ever want to jeopardise it. 'But I *am* a king and have been for some time,' he said softly. 'You knew that. So nothing has changed, Francesca.'

Frankie stared into the gleaming depths of his ebony eyes. 'Yes, intellectually I knew all that. But seeing it for myself is a little dazzling—the robes and the palace and the servants. I'm used to seeing a more casual version of you back in England.'

He picked up a grape and ate it. 'If it makes

you feel any better, it's pretty strange for me to have a woman sitting here like this.'

'But there must have been women here before,' she probed.

'Very occasionally, yes—of course—but they are always married women, accompanying their husbands. Never…' *Never a woman whose scent of rose and jasmine was filling his senses.* 'A single woman,' he finished unevenly.

'So no.' Go on, she urged herself fiercely. *Say it!* Acknowledge the reality of his life instead of your own wishful fantasy version of it. 'No girlfriends?' she finished, as carelessly as she could.

He shook his head. 'Certainly not—for I would consider that disrespectful. I indulge my very natural appetites when I am abroad, never here, and always in the utmost privacy. One day, of course, I will marry. And then my bed will be shared by my….wife.'

The question she'd asked and the answer she'd dreaded now caused her pain, but somehow

Frankie's polite smile didn't slip. 'You seem to have your future all mapped out.'

'Of course. It comes with the territory.' He shrugged. 'Though in a way, it is easy for me. I do not have the luxury of choice—for it is my destiny. I will take a wife of pure Khayarzahian stock and thus ensure the continuation of the noble bloodline.'

'But isn't that a little...*old-fashioned*?'

He ate another grape, his teeth biting into the flesh, and a little rush of juice sweetened his mouth. 'More than a little—but I do not take issue with that. I am, as has been acknowledged many times, an old-fashioned man. It is the way things are here and, besides, much of modern life is flawed—you know that as well as I do, Francesca.'

'So you don't resent it?' she questioned, as some vital need to know drove her on. 'The fact that for you there *is* no choice—that you must take a bride who is expected of you, rather than choosing one of your own free will?'

His eyes glittered as he leaned back against the

mound of brocade cushions. 'There is no point in railing against the inevitable. And choice can be a poisoned chalice,' he added softly. 'It inspires greed and makes people discontented with their lot. Couples seek perfection in relationships, something which is simply not possible—and when that perfection fails to materialise, they go looking for it elsewhere. Look at your divorce rate in the west and ask yourself whether choice is such a good thing.'

It was not the answer that Frankie had secretly been hoping for—for wasn't it true that deep down she had *wanted* him to rail against his fate? To shake an angry fist at the empty air and admit that he longed to follow his heart. But he had done the very opposite and had sounded as if he meant every word of it. She bit her lip as she stared down at her hands, which lay clasped in her lap. Because surely she wasn't stupid enough to consider herself a candidate for his heart?

'And besides,' he continued softly, 'I will make sure that my bride is beautiful, as well as suitable—so it will be no hardship to spend my life with her.'

The truth hurt, she realised—it hurt like crazy.

She raised her head to look at him. His face was illuminated by the light from the lamps and his high cheekbones cast angled shadows upon his burnished skin. And suddenly she wanted the evening to end and to be alone with her aching heart in the privacy of her room. 'Am I supposed to wait until you retire—or am I allowed to go to bed now?' she asked.

Silently, Zahid cursed her question, wondering if it was as innocent as it sounded—for he knew a million women who would have asked it with something other than sleep on their minds. 'You are tired?' he queried coolly.

'Very.' She kept her voice brisk, knowing that this was how it was going to have to be. She was going to have to remain crisp and bright and professional—and bury all those stupid romantic dreams once and for all. 'It's been a long day.'

'Indeed it has.' Gracefully, he rose to his feet in a shimmer of silk, shaking his head emphatically at one of the servants who immediately stepped forward. He rapped out an order in his native tongue before gesturing to Francesca. 'Come, I will take you there myself.'

Smoothing down her tunic, Frankie scrambled to her feet. 'There's no need for you to do that, Zahid.'

'There is every need—for you will only lose yourself in the vast corridors of my palace,' he drawled, without stopping to ask himself why he had not let the servant accompany her.

Their footfall and the soft swish of Zahid's robes brushing over the marble floor were the only sounds to be heard as they made their way through the long passageways. That and the loud thunder of Frankie's heart as she followed him.

She forced herself to register landmarks along the way even though the arching pillars and intricate mosaics all looked very similar. And then Zahid came to a halt by her room and turned, his eyes glittering ebony in the dim light.

'Here we are. Safely delivered to your door.'

'Thank you very much.' But she didn't feel

safe as she stared up into the hawklike features and the lash-framed shards of his black eyes. She felt…what? As if danger and excitement were shimmering in the air around them, as tangible as any aura. One step and she could be in his arms, locked in the powerful circle of his embrace. And wasn't that what she yearned for—the culmination of all those years of wistful longing?

Afterwards, she wondered if she communicated something of her desire to him—for why else did he lift his hand to her cheek and lay it there, like a blessing?

'Goodnight, Francesca,' he said softly.

'Goodnight,' she whispered back. The warmth of his hand against her skin was beguiling and she turned her head, just by a fraction—but enough for her lips to graze against his palm. It hadn't been intentional—or at least, she didn't think it was—but it was enough to make him expel a sudden, shuddering breath of air.

'Are you trying to test my resolve?' he demanded unsteadily, but he left his hand exactly where it was and he could feel the warmth of her breath against his skin as she mouthed a single word.

'No.'

Slowly, his thumb began to trace the trembling outline of her lips. 'I'm not sure that I believe you.'

'I'm no…no…liar, Zahid.'

'No.' He knew that. But suddenly he wanted her to be. He wanted her to be devious and manipulative so that his conscience would allow him to pull her into his arms and start making love to her. He wanted her to be *something*— something other than this fresh-faced and blue-eyed girl he'd known for ever, who was making him feel a desire he had no earthly right to feel.

He gave a low laugh as he tilted her face upwards, but his mood was dark as well as anticipatory for deep down he knew this was wrong. *And shouldn't he be the one to stop it—stop it now, before it was too late?*

'Zahid?'

Her tentative question crept into the stillness of the night and hung there.

'Maybe we should stop torturing ourselves and just give into the inevitable,' he bit out. 'Because what's the point of fighting something neither of us has the heart to fight?' And without giving her a chance to respond, he pulled her into his arms and drove his mouth down on hers in a kiss which had been much too long in the waiting.

Caught off guard by the heated pressure of his lips, Frankie swayed, but he pulled her even closer, so that she could feel the hardness of his body and the wild beat of his heart through the silk of his robes. She should have been daunted by all that unashamed masculinity—but somehow she wasn't. How could she be when he was kissing her with a passion which was overwhelming her—*swamping* her with a rush of pure pleasure? Simon had never made her feel like *this*.

She felt both weak and strong—any lingering doubts vanquished by the sheer potency of Zahid's hungry male body as it pressed against hers. It was as if she'd accidentally fallen into a stream and been taken up by a powerful current—then finding that she was too helpless to fight against it. *And she didn't want to fight against it. She wanted this, and more of this. More of him.*

'Z-Zahid.' With another breathless moan, Frankie reached up—wanting to tangle her fingers in the thick darkness of his hair. But his head was covered and as her fingers met the barrier of his headdress they halted there—unsure of what to do next.

Zahid froze. The soft yielding of her body was intoxicating—but a woman touching his headdress was a rare enough action to make him jerk back and stop kissing her. He only ever made love in western clothes, he realised—and the irony of that didn't escape him. For once he would not have the tiresome unzipping of trousers and unbuttoning of shirts—because the loose form of his silken robes would allow him almost instant access to her...

And for once it was not going to happen...

Reaching up, he caught hold of her hand and pulled it away from his head, aware of the pulse which hammered so frantically through the delicate skin at her wrist. What had he been *thinking* of? Did all the noble pronouncements he'd made about women at dinner count for nothing?

Yet as he stared down at the disappointed trembling of her lips he recognised how easy it would be to take her. One swift and seamless derobement and he could be deep inside her, driving into her moist warmth and spilling his seed. Was she as easy as this for all men? he wondered, his mouth tightening with fury.

'This wasn't supposed to happen!' he ground out as he took a step away from her.

Distractedly, she nodded—aware of the soft pooling of desire which was making her feel as weak as a kitten. 'No, I know it wasn't,' she whispered. 'B-but—'

'No buts, Francesca,' he put in fiercely. 'Definitely no buts.' With an angry growl, he opened the bedroom door, his hands infinitely more gentle than his words.

'Just go to sleep,' he said roughly—and with that, Zahid pushed her inside the gilded bedroom and firmly closed the door behind her.

CHAPTER NINE

'So WHERE exactly are we going?' Frankie injected what she thought was just the right amount of polite interest into her voice as she sat back in the passenger seat of the enormous four-wheel drive.

To hell and back, thought Zahid grimly. Sharply, he turned the key in the ignition and eased away into the shining brightness of the desert morning. 'To the new horse-racing stadium, so that you can see it for yourself before you start work on the diaries. I want you to give me your opinion on how well you think the women's facilities are being catered for—as honestly as only you can, Frankie.'

Great, thought Frankie, blinking her eyes furiously behind the welcome covering of her shades, not knowing if she was trying to hold off tears or tiredness. You get rejected by yet another man and spend a long sleepless night thinking about him—and then he tells you that your day will be spent inspecting the 'women's facilities' at Khayarzah's new racing track. It really didn't get much worse than that, did it?

'Fine with me.' Forcing a neutral smile, she risked a glance at the hawklike profile and hard, unsmiling lips. 'Why are you driving—and not one of your chauffeurs?'

Zahid's hands tightened on the steering wheel. Why did she think he was driving? Wasn't it obvious? To give him something to do other than give into the temptation of finishing off what they'd started last night. Something to look at other than the soft temptation of her lips and thinking about where on his body he would like them to be placed. He glanced in his mirror to see the dark shape of the security car behind, which was shadowing them.

'I like to drive. Especially in the desert. The roads are flat and straight and you can put your foot right down in a way you can't do anywhere else in the world.'

'Right.' Frankie settled back in her seat. Think positive, she told herself. Don't let him realise that you're hurting, or that you can't stop thinking about the hot brush of his lips and the way he made you feel when he held you in his arms last night. She forced herself to concentrate on the road ahead. 'Well, I quite like driving myself— so maybe later on, I can have a go.'

There was the split second of a pause. 'I'm afraid that won't be possible,' he said pleasantly.

'Really? I'm sure that as Sheikh you can get me emergency cover on your car insurance, Zahid.'

He bit back a reluctant smile. 'It's nothing to do with the insurance. It's a very powerful machine.'

If she hadn't been feeling so pent-up and rejected she might have just let that go. But now Frankie was pleased to have something to concentrate on other than the fact that for the first time in her life she was experiencing an intense kind of frustration.

'Fortunately I passed my driving test on the first attempt,' she said sweetly. 'And not just the section for "delicate little women who shouldn't be allowed behind the wheel of a big car".' A new sense of determination filled her. 'So I'd like to have a go at driving, if that's all right with you.'

'Actually, it is not,' he said, flexing his fingers as he anticipated her reaction to his next statement. 'I'm afraid women aren't allowed to drive in my country.'

This time the pause was longer. 'You *are* kidding?'

He shot her a glance. Today she was wearing a tunic and trousers in ice-blue—a cool and untouchable contrast to the hot question which burst from her lips. 'No, I'm not.'

'Women aren't allowed to drive?' she verified, and when he gave a terse nod she raked her fingers back through her hair in agitation. 'Why not?'

Zahid's hands tightened around the steering wheel. He had brought her here to type his father's diaries—not to challenge him or the laws of his land!

'Don't ask me, the laws have been in place for decades.' Frankie's lips fell open as she turned her head to look at him.

'I keep thinking that you're going to come out with some sort of punchline and tell me that it's some kind of joke.'

'I know it seems outdated to you—and to me in fact. But the previous sheikh was not a moderniser. His view—which is still shared by many—was that men and women should not mix freely. At the moment it's just the way things are.'

'I realise that now—and I assume that's the same reason you won't let women go to university.' She saw him nod his head before turning on him angrily. 'But *why* would you stop women from mixing freely with men?'

'Because it is felt that women need to be protected.'

'From who—or what, exactly?'

'From men, of course—and from themselves!'

'And you call that protection?' Frankie shook her head. 'Some people might reasonably describe it as a kind of prison.'

'It depends on your point of view.' Zahid put his foot down on the accelerator. 'Proximity equals sex—and sex before marriage isn't always a good thing. You should know that better than anyone, Francesca—since the man to whom you gave yourself is no longer a part of your future. What a waste of time *that* was.'

If he hadn't made her so angry then she might have told him that he was leaping to false conclusions. As it was, his arrogant statement so irked her that she turned the accusation on *him*.

'So you go away on your foreign trips and have as much sex as you want, on the clear understanding that you will one day return home to marry a Khayarzahian virgin?' she demanded as a hot little spear of jealousy lanced through her like a sabre.

He shrugged. 'I am now the king,' he said quietly. 'And that is what is expected of me.'

And despite knowing that he was a victim of

his own circumstances, Frankie could not bite back her burning sense of injustice. 'Meaning that it's one rule for men and another for women?'

He looked in his rear mirror. 'I'm afraid so,' he answered, softly. 'And it has always been that way, no matter how much the feminists might protest.'

Frankie stared out of the window as the car shot along the long and straight desert road and tried to quell her rising tide of indignation. What century did he think he was he living in?

'Well, if men and women should not be mixing freely in Khayarzah—then why on earth did you bring me here?'

Behind his shades, Zahid's eyes narrowed as the roads became fringed with towering date trees, and he slowed down to pass a horse-drawn cart which contained sacks of rice. He felt the familiar flicker of lust licking at his groin. 'You think I haven't already asked myself that very question and realised that I was mistaken in doing so?'

'In what way mistaken?' she flashed back.

For a moment, he didn't answer. But was there any point in pretending, after what had happened last night? One stupid little kiss which had dominated his thoughts ever since, no matter how hard he tried to push it aside. One kiss which had made him wonder whether there was any point in holding back any more. One kiss which had kept him hard and aching all night long and which was making him hard right now... 'Thinking that I could resist you. That resisting you would be a useful test in self-control.'

'But you *did* resist me,' she pointed out. 'So you've passed your stupid test.'

He gave a short laugh. 'I can't believe I'm having this conversation with you.'

'Neither can I.' But even as she said it Frankie realised that it wasn't quite true. Because despite the fundamental disagreements which lay at the heart of their heated discussion, she was aware of an intimacy which existed between her and Zahid, which had never been there with Simon. Was that because she'd known the sheikh for so many years that she felt she could be *herself* with him, no matter how huge the differences in their circumstances? Because she'd known him as a *person* before this inconvenient sexual attraction had reared its seductive head?

'Look over there,' he said suddenly. 'We are skirting the outskirts of Calathara, which is our second biggest city—famous for its diamonds and carpets and the sweetest oranges on the planet. And if you look carefully you'll see the stadium in the distance.'

She was relieved to be able to change the subject and as they approached the stadium it was difficult not to be impressed by the amount of money and work which had clearly been poured into the new building. A gleam of chrome and glass rose up to greet them and Frankie studied the sleek design as she stepped from the car to greet the now-familiar deputation which awaited them.

Walking just behind Zahid, she marvelled at the state-of-the-art racetrack, whose lush grass track curved like an emerald snake—made all the more startling by its stark desert location. She'd once gone to a Boxing Day race meeting in England with her father—but the racecourse had been nothing like this.

Here, no expense had been spared. Not anywhere. Everything was brand-new and the very best that money could buy. There were dining rooms and function rooms—as well as fabulous facilities for the horses and their jockeys. The women's section was separate and lavish, filled with beautiful containers of showy orchids, and there was a dazzling array of French perfumes and soaps in the washrooms.

In one of the executive dining rooms, they drank strong, sweet coffee from dinky little cups and ate cake which had been flavoured with honey and cardamom. And Frankie thought how animated and proud Zahid seemed as they sipped at their coffee.

'I want to make this track part of the international circuit,' he said. 'And for the Khayarzah Cup to be one of the most treasured trophies of the twenty-first century—on a par with the prizes offered at Ascot and Cheltenham and Melbourne.' He put down his cup and looked at her. 'So what do you think of it?

'I think it's superb.'

Zahid gave a satisfied smile. 'It is, isn't it?'

'I also think it's a contradiction.'

His eyes narrowed. 'I'm sorry?'

Frankie wondered whether she would have been saying all this if he'd come into her room last night and made love to her. Would she have been quite so keen to find fault if that had been the case? But it wasn't *fault*, she told herself fiercely. It was a legitimate opinion—and one which he had asked for.

She clasped her hands together. 'You're hoping to attract an international clientele?'

'Of course. It won't work without one.'

'Well, I can tell you right now, Zahid, that independent women will not tolerate being forbidden to drive. How are you proposing they get around?'

'There will be taxis. Chauffeurs.' He gave a soft laugh. 'Show me a woman who doesn't like having a driver—though I doubt you will be able to produce one.'

Impatiently, she shook her head. 'You're missing the point. Women may like being chauffeured around but they will see the driving ban as completely unreasonable. They won't want their liberty being curtailed.'

'Then let them stay away!'

'Meaning their powerful husbands might stay away, too—and then where will you be? You won't have successful horse races if you're playing to an empty stadium!'

Zahid tensed. Why had he thought that bringing her out here was a good idea? It was supposed to be as a favour to *her*—to give her a break after the demise of her disastrous relationship. And yes, he had tailor-made a job for her, but for that he expected her unquestioning loyalty. He certainly hadn't expected to have to endure a tirade of criticism. A nerve flickered at his temple. 'You are perfectly entitled to your opinion, Francesca. Just don't expect me to agree with it.'

'So you only employ people who tell you what you want to hear?' she suggested softly.

Zahid stilled. Enough was enough! Why, he was according her all kinds of privilege and yet she could not show him even a modicum of common courtesy! He stood up.

'Let's go,' he said abruptly.

She knew he was angry, but she didn't care; she was angry herself—she just wasn't sure why. Or maybe she was and she didn't want to admit it.

She heard him saying something terse in his native tongue to the bodyguards who had followed them and then, having made their farewells to the various dignitaries, the two of them made their way to the car in complete silence.

As the car pulled away Frankie stared out of the window at the startlingly clear line of the distant horizon and deep blue of the desert sky. She saw the sizzle of heat shimmering off the sand and wondered why her heart felt as if it had been plunged into ice-water.

Beside her, Zahid simmered with unspoken rage as he drove and she was aware that she was witnessing a very royal *sulk*. Well, let him sulk! And did he really have to drive that fast?

'You're driving very fast, Zahid.'

'And?'

She bit back a smile at his unashamed arrogance—and yet that made her even angrier. She didn't *want* to smile. She wanted to… Her fingertips strayed to her mouth.

'Don't bite your nails, Francesca.'

'Why, are women forbidden to do *that*, as well?'

He swallowed. She really *was* outrageous. Feisty and fearless and not afraid to say what was on her mind. Shifting a little, he tried in vain to dispel some of the dull ache he felt deep in his groin. He was aware of her own body language, which was making her sit so rigidly in the passenger seat, even if he hadn't been able to detect the steadily escalating sexual tension in the air around them.

Out of the corner of his eye, he could see her cross one slim and silk-clad leg over the other and, no matter how hard he tried, he couldn't prevent himself from imagining her naked. What would her nipples be like? he wondered distractedly. Like tiny, puckered rose-buds crowning a soft and creamy breast? Or large pale pink discs which he could slowly encircle with his tongue?

His erotic imaginings proved too much and suddenly the barriers he had erected between them came tumbling down. His fingers gripped the steering wheel as his mind and his body went to war. Who was he trying to protect by not making love to her—when she was clearly a feisty woman who had made it plain that she despised inequality?

She didn't *want* protection. She wanted him.

And he wanted her.

He glanced in the driving mirror to see the tail-car behind them and as he pressed down hard on the accelerator he saw it begin to retreat until it was nothing more than a tiny black dot in the distance.

He drove with a new sense of purpose, the powerful vehicle eating up the undemanding miles of the desert road, until at last he turned left, down a small track lined with tall cacti, and Frankie was certain that she could see the distant gleam of water in the distance.

Her forehead creased in a frown and she felt the sudden prickling of her skin. 'Where...where are we going, Zahid?'

He recognised that it was a loaded question—and he was careful not to be evasive as he slowed the car down. She should have the opportunity to reject him, even if he knew, deep down, that she wasn't going to.

'I have my own, private house nearby. It's where I go to escape sometimes.' He paused, meaningfully. 'I thought you might like to see it.'

Something in the silky darkness of his tone washed over her senses and Frankie's heart began to hammer as she recognised the unmistakable desire which underpinned his question. This wasn't a guided tour of one of his properties he was offering—his intention was made perfectly clear by the hot sparking of his black eyes.

For a moment she felt intensely vulnerable—

but the feeling quickly melted away as she recognised that this opportunity might never come again. That this was the culmination of all her dreams. She bit her lip. She had wanted Zahid for as long as she could remember—and years of wistful fantasy now stood a chance of coming true.

'I'd love to see it,' she said steadily.

CHAPTER TEN

THERE was no finesse. No honeyed words which preceded a leisurely and sophisticated seduction. There was barely even time to take in the surprisingly modern building—for no sooner had the door of Zahid's private house closed behind them than he pulled Frankie into his arms. For a moment, his hands framed her face as he looked down into the wide-spaced blue eyes and the high colour which was splashed over her cheekbones.

'Francesca,' he grated. 'God help me for doing this.'

'Then God help me, too,' she whispered.

And then they were in each other's arms and kissing as if it had just been invented. Only for Frankie, maybe it just had—because no kiss could ever have prepared her for *this*. Her arms wrapped themselves tightly around his neck and she clung to him like some kind of rampant vine while their mouths locked and their tongues played intimate little dances. With a groan, he pulled her closer into his body. She could feel the hot throb of his need pressing urgently against her and, although she should have found it daunting, it did nothing but make her wriggle her body impatiently against his.

With an effort, he tore himself away from her and saw the dark bewilderment in her eyes.

'What is it?' she whispered.

He shook his head. 'Not here. Come with me. I want to do this properly.'

Properly. It was a word steeped in both sensuality and formality and Frankie gave a shiver of anticipation as he took her hand in his and led her into a room off the main area which was dominated by an enormous bed. She was dimly aware of an extraordinary light from outside—which was quickly muted when Zahid pressed a button recessed into one of the walls and blinds floated down to blot out the day.

'Now...' Lifting his hands, he tangled his fingers in the satin spill of her dark hair and could feel the soft butt of her breasts as he pulled her close to kiss her again. And it was torture. The sweetest and most exquisite torture he could imagine. If it had been anyone else, he would have taken her swiftly and left the slow lovemaking until afterwards, when his urgent hunger had been satisfied. But he did not want to take her like that. Not Francesca. He wanted to do it slow and he wanted her naked. To see every glorious inch of her.

'Let's rid ourselves of these damned clothes, shall we?'

Frankie's heart was racing as he brushed his lips negligently over hers. Half of her was afraid to let him go—terrified that he might change his mind and decide that his wretched self-control was more important than this. But the old familiar nerves which she had been dreading had so far failed to make an appearance. 'Oh, Zahid,' she whispered. 'Yes, please.'

With one movement and the swift gleam of a

smile, he tore off his headdress—to reveal the familiar raven-blue gleam of his hair. 'Lift up your arms,' he said unsteadily.

Where were all those paralysing insecurities now? she wondered. Banished by the urgency of her desire for him, that was where. She did as he commanded, so that he was able to skim off her tunic, and then the silken trousers were removed in one fluid movement. She realised that her mediocre bra and panties were on show and that maybe this was the point where she should have felt self-conscious. Yet the hot look of approbation which glittered from his eyes made her thrill with a potent kind of pride and suddenly she forgot the fact that she was wearing chain-store underwear.

Impatiently, he pulled off his own clothing and suddenly Frankie felt a wave of shyness as she realised that he was completely naked beneath it. The robes fell to the ground in a whisper and her cheeks flamed as she saw the hard, lean body and the proud evidence of his arousal.

'You like what you see?' he murmured.

Too dazed to speak, she nodded her head, even though she was certainly no expert. But she liked what she saw in Zahid's body—all burnished skin covering honed and powerful muscle. More importantly, she liked the man inside it—in spite of his outrageously outdated attitudes and cavalier air.

Her skin and her body felt as if they were on fire as, impatiently, he pushed aside a cashmere throw and drew her down onto the smooth, satin surface of the bed.

'Zahid...' She closed her eyes as he peeled off her bra and panties and brought her close to his naked body.

'Mmm?'

'It's...' His fingers were tiptoeing over her breasts—teasing the achingly aroused and puckered nipples and then letting his palms spread deliciously over them, covering them like a warm blanket.

'What is it, *anisah bahiya*?' he murmured. 'Is it like a little piece of heaven that we have found here on earth?'

'Yes, *yes*—that's exactly it! Oh! Oh!' Now his lips were on her breasts and his fingers were snaking their way down over her belly as the feeling of warmth grew into one of molten heat.

She should have felt shy when he touched her where she most longed to be touched, but how could she be shy about entering the little piece of heaven he had so rightly described? And should she be touching *him*? What would a man like Zahid expect from his lover?

Tentatively, her fingertips reached down to brush against his manhood. It felt like silk and steel, she thought, before her hand was swiftly removed from his flesh as if she had been caught pick-pocketing.

'No, *anisah*,' he murmured regretfully as he kissed each finger in turn. 'Not this time—for you have made me so aroused that I do not trust myself. I am like a novice in your arms and if you touch me again like that, it will all be over.' It was, he realised with a sudden start, the most intimate thing he had ever said to a woman. But his thoughts reminded him of one vital omission and he reached into the cabinet beside the bed to extract a condom, stroking it on with a strange and unmistakable reluctance. And there was a conversation he still needed to have with her...

He moved over her, his arousal pressing provocatively between her thighs, but he forced himself to say what he knew he owed her, even if it meant that the mood might be destroyed and the moment lost for ever.

'Francesca...'

Her eyes fluttered open in question; she was terrified that he might be about to change his mind. 'What?'

'It is not the right time to say this—and yet if I wait, it will be too late.'

'S-say what?'

'You...you do not expect this to lead to something permanent?' he questioned unevenly. 'Because it can never be. You do realise that?'

Frankie stared up into the shifting shadows of his face, momentarily cursing his sense of timing. The heartbreaking words left her in no doubt of his feelings for her, but that didn't

change a thing. 'Of course I don't. I just want...'
What did she want? To feel as other women
felt? To experience pleasure with a man she had
always adored? Should she tell him the secret she
had kept buttoned up inside her? She looked up
at the bowed outline of his lips—so close that
she could feel the warmth of his breath on her
face.

And if she told him, then what? Would he stop?
Yes, she realised, with an instinct she instantly
trusted. He *would* stop. Even if it took a supreme
effort of will which would defeat most men—
Zahid would somehow manage it.

'What do you want, Francesca?' he murmured.

No. She would not tell him. At least, not yet.
'I want...*you.*'

'Then you shall have me.' His lips grazed
hers as he moved over her, his fingers moving
between her thighs to part her moist flesh in
readiness. Grasping his manhood, he brushed
provocatively against her honeyed heat. 'You
shall have me right...*now.*'

Urgently, he thrust inside her—but the warning bells rang too late. It happened before Zahid properly realised what was happening—before his disbelieving senses could piece together all the facts. The brief barrier. The momentary resistance to his deep thrust before he broke through into a place of such sweet, wet tightness that he groaned aloud. The tiny whimpering sound of pain she made confirmed his worst suspicions but by then it was too late and anger melded with passion and became an unstoppable mix.

'Zahid!' She gave a soft gasp as he tightened his hold on her.

'Relax,' he instructed throatily as he began to move inside her. 'Let go.'

'Oh, Zahid,' she said again, more brokenly this time.

He'd never known love-making like it—even though it tested every reserve he possessed. Time and time he held back from giving into his orgasm—determined that her first time would be memorable for the right reasons. Or at least *some* of the right reasons, he thought grimly as his fingers gripped the satin of her thighs to drive into her even deeper.

Her head turned wildly against the pillow as she began to make soft, moaning sounds—and when at last he sensed the change in her, he drew back to watch it happen. Saw the slow arching of her back and the rosy flowering over her breasts. Heard the fevered entreaty gasped from her parted lips as her orgasm captured her.

Even before her spasms had stilled, he sensed the inevitability of his own release and felt it like nothing he had ever felt before. Everything paled in comparison to those fleeting moments of pure pleasure. Every milestone of his life, every battle fought and victory won—he would have traded them all for this one moment of delicious weakness with Francesca O'Hara.

But afterwards, when his body had begun to quieten, his thoughts began to race. Slowly, he withdrew from her—taking a moment to compose himself before turning her towards him, steeling his heart against the trickle of a tear which slid down her cheek.

It was long moments before he could bring himself to speak and when he did, his words shot out like bullets. The only woman he had thought he could trust—and she had deceived him in the most fundamental way of all.

'So,' he said heavily. 'Are you going to give me some kind of explanation?'

She heard the sudden coolness in his voice and Frankie's heart sank as some of her joy began to evaporate. Couldn't the interrogation wait? Couldn't he just let her revel in this feeling—let her enjoy the sense of warmth and closeness she was experiencing right now? Surely she was allowed to spin out her hopeless fantasies about her dark and brooding lover for just a little longer.

'You mean about—'

'Please don't make it worse by playing games with me, Francesca. It seems you've done enough game-playing to last a lifetime.' Angrily, he wiped away the tear which shimmered on her cheek and which seemed to reproach him. Why hadn't she told him before it was too late? 'You know exactly what I mean.'

'About me being…' Her voice tailed off because the word seemed like an unwanted intruder and the dark look on his face filled her with trepidation.

'A virgin. A *virgin*!' He shook his head in disbelief as he rolled away from her, reaching down to grab the cashmere throw, which had tumbled to the floor during their love-making and thrusting it at her, not wanting to look at her pink and white nakedness. He saw her move one milky thigh to reveal the secret, dark fuzz of hair and felt the rapid escalation of his heart. 'Cover yourself up!'

Frankie was grateful for the blanket, tugging it over herself with trembling fingers as she stared at him with apprehensive eyes.

'Why didn't you tell me?' he demanded.

'Because I knew you would stop if I did—'

'Damned right I would have stopped!'

'And I didn't want you to,' she said, in a small voice.

Her wide-eyed honesty took him aback and almost made him melt, until he reminded himself of what she had done and the repercussions of her actions. 'You didn't have sex with Simon?' he queried, then gave a short laugh as he realised the ridiculous nature of his question. 'Clearly not, as I've just discovered for myself.' He looked at her, trying to steel himself against the softness of her lips and the blue temptation of her darkened eyes. 'The question is, why not?'

She felt as if she were on a witness stand—suddenly expected to mount her own defence with little or no preparation. And her only defence was the truth, Frankie realised—even if it opened her up to the charge of being too trusting and too vulnerable.

'Because I was...*nervous* whenever Simon touched me.' Awkwardly, she wriggled her shoulders. 'I sort of...*froze.*'

'You didn't act very nervous just now.' And she certainly hadn't frozen.

She swallowed but the candid question still sparked from his black eyes. Did he want her to spell it out for him, detail by cringe-making detail—and inflate his already over-inflated ego into the bargain? Did she admit that she'd been stupid enough to get engaged to a man who hadn't made her feel a modicum of what she felt for the brooding sheikh? That she had only just discovered what real passion and desire could feel like?

'You made me feel relaxed,' she said simply. 'No, maybe that's the wrong word. You made me feel...' She gave another rueful shrug of her shoulders—for surely there was no place for coyness now. 'Wanton, I guess. Which he never did. He told me that day when I went to see him that I was basically...frigid. And I believed him.' She stopped while Zahid said something very profound in his native tongue, her heart beating hopefully as he pulled the cashmere throw over him as well, so that she could feel the heat from his body as he drew closer. 'Anyway, maybe I should be grateful that we didn't have sex.' Her voice wobbled a little. 'Not if he was sleeping with somebody else at the time.'

Zahid gave a ragged sigh as he stared at the ceiling, cursing the man who had hurt her and cursing his own hot-blooded impetuosity. How bloody complicated life could be at times, he thought. The best sex he'd ever had and it had been with his oldest friend—who had now wasted her virginity on him and given him a whole new layer of unwanted responsibility towards her. Was this not the most impossible of all situations?

'You know what kind of man I am, Francesca,' he said furiously. 'As King, I will be expected to marry a virgin—but it will have to be a woman from my own culture,' he ran on hastily, in case she should think that she now qualified for the position. 'Not a foreigner.'

Frankie was glad that he was looking at the ceiling because otherwise he might have seen the hurt which had criss-crossed over her face. How unwittingly cruel he could be. Did he think she was now angling for marriage, simply because he had been the first man she'd had sex with? Did he imagine that she had withheld the information from him in order to put herself in a powerful position?

But it took her only moments to compose herself. Why *should* he feel guilt about what had just happened, when in a way—she *had* misled him? Yet she hadn't kept quiet about her innocence because she had some form of agenda. She had done it because she'd wanted Zahid more than anything else in the world. She had wanted him to be the man to introduce her to the world of sex. And she had done it because she…well, she *liked* him. That was all. Surely that was something which could be celebrated instead of regretted?

Beneath the superfine cashmere, she stretched her glowing body and the movement made him turn his head to look at her, his eyes narrowing as she gave him a tentative smile.

'I don't want to fall out about it,' she said softly, and with that she reached out her hand to cup the jut of his jaw. She could feel the rasp of new growth there and traced her thumb over his lips, not surprised when he caught it between his teeth and gave it a tiny nip.

'Neither do I,' he growled.

'So couldn't we…couldn't we forget it ever happened?'

'Are you crazy?' The absurdity of her statement stirred him into action and he rolled closer, pulling her against his warm and newly aroused body. And then he sighed. 'No, you're just inexperienced—and in a way, it's a bit of a pity that you've started with the best.'

She bristled at the implication behind his words. 'You mean that no lover will ever match you?'

That hadn't been what he'd meant at all. He'd meant that sex rarely felt this good—especially given that it was her first time. He wondered why that was, before quickly dismissing the thought. The whys and wherefores were irrelevant—it was the facts they had to deal with. And the fact was that he had just made love to his sweet virginal Francesca and he wanted to do it again.

'I doubt it,' he told her honestly.

'Why, you arrogant—'

He silenced her with the brush of his lips.

'Arrogance is sometimes the truth, *anisah*,' he said sombrely.

When he spoke like that—how could she resist him? When his black eyes looked as deep and as dark as ink and she just wanted to write her name with them…

'Oh, Zahid.'

'Zahid, what?'

She shook her head, shrugged her shoulders helplessly so that the throw slipped down. 'I don't know,' she whispered.

And neither did he. All he could think about was the distracting softness of her warm breasts and her evocative feminine scent, which seemed to have invaded his senses. His lips brushing against her shoulder, he slid his fingers between her thighs as he gave into a temptation he had no desire to resist. Why mar this beautiful experience with troublesome questions which could easily wait?

Lowering his mouth onto hers, he gave a low moan as his kiss blotted everything except the hungry clamour of their bodies.

CHAPTER ELEVEN

THE finger which was stroking circles on her belly suddenly stilled and Frankie made a little sound which was midway between pleasure and protest.

'That's nice,' she whispered.

'I know it is. Too damned nice.' With a quick and disbelieving glance at his watch, Zahid saw that it was two hours since they had left the racing stadium. Two hours which hadn't been scheduled into his busy itinerary, which had been spent exploring her sweet body. With an effort, he pushed aside the covers and forced himself to get out of bed and away from the warm lure of her arms. For a woman who was new to sex she had certainly embraced it with enthusiasm. He had never imagined that she could be so deliciously *imaginative*.

'We can't lie around in bed any longer, Francesca—my bodyguards will be wondering what the hell I am doing.'

His mouth hardened. Actually, they would probably have a pretty good idea of what he was doing, he realised—and it was his own stupid fault. He had broken all the rules by bringing Francesca to his private house and spending the whole afternoon making love to her.

'Zahid—'

'Not now. We'd better get dressed and on our way.' Brutally, his words cut across hers—he was terrified that she might make another breathy little sound, which would compel him to start exploring her hot and tight little body yet again. He stared down at her, naked on his bed. Dark hair spilled over her shoulders and her creamy thighs were parted indolently—and with a small groan he swallowed down his rising lust and backed away. 'Will you stop tempting me?' he demanded.

'But I'm not doing anything!'

Now was not the time to explain that she was

managing to make him more aroused than he could ever remember feeling before. Because how could he possibly explain something he didn't understand? Instead, he forced his mind to practicalities. 'I'm afraid that we're going to have to wait until we get back to the palace to shower—if you can bear to.' Because they might as well have taken out a full-page advertisement in the *Khayarzah Times* if they suddenly reappeared with damp hair and flushed faces. Even if it meant that the return journey would be perfumed with the distinctive scent of sex. 'Francesca, will you *please* get up?'

Reluctantly, Frankie did as he asked—acutely aware of the fact that she was stark-naked in front of a man she'd known all her life. It felt strange to be getting dressed in such a bizarre setting—and stranger still to see Zahid, his back now averted, hurriedly pulling on his robes.

Locating her bag and finding a nearby bathroom, she freshened up as best she could. But when she returned to the bedroom, it was to find Zahid looking grim—and suddenly, her heart sank with a sense of dread. Was he going to tell her something she suspected he'd felt all along—that he'd just made the biggest mistake of his life?

'So…what happens now?' she asked in a small voice.

Expelling a sigh, he shook his head. If it had been anyone but Francesca, it would have been easy. He could have kissed and dismissed her with a promise to look her up when he was back in London. And then put her on the next plane home and forgotten all about her.

But it wasn't anyone else—and the very fact that it was Francesca was what made the whole situation so damned difficult. He had brought her here to give her a chance to forget her problems back in England—and had promptly added to those problems a hundredfold, by seducing her! *And to make matters worse, she had given him her virginity—the greatest gift a woman could give her lover. Wouldn't that make her clingy—even clingier than new lovers so often were?*

He needed to play it down. To show her that

nothing need change. That their friendship could remain intact, if they handled it properly. 'We might be able to manage the situation,' he said slowly. 'If we are very careful.'

Frankie looked at him, fearing the worst—for she had seen the calculating expression which had suddenly hardened his features. 'Manage it?' she echoed cautiously.

He stared at the soft pink face she'd just washed and knew that he had to be straight with her. 'We've just crossed a forbidden line by making love,' he said.

Lips pursed, she nodded, even though he made it sound as if they'd committed some sort of *trespass*. 'I realise that.'

'And I ought to send you back to England straight away—for both our sakes.' He saw her face working as she tried desperately not to react to his words and he found himself wondering if his own reaction was mirroring hers. Could she sense his own reluctance to do that?

'But the thing is, that I don't want to send you back.'

A new note of hope entered her voice. 'You don't?'

'No. I want you to type up my father's diaries as planned.' He swallowed. 'And I want to carry on making love to you.'

'You...do?'

'Of course I do,' he growled. His eyes met hers, and he felt another urgent leap of desire as he registered her quick rise in colour. 'Isn't it crazy for us not to enjoy each other for a little longer?'

Frankie's cheeks burned and her heart raced. She agreed with every word he said, yet she wished he hadn't approached it quite so cold-bloodedly. Couldn't he have just pulled her into his arms and told her between urgent kisses that he couldn't bear to let her go—rather than making it sound like something which was on the agenda at a board meeting?

But Frankie recognised that it was an indication of Zahid's sense of decency that he was not blinding her with emotion, or trying to sway her with more glorious sex. He was putting an offer on the table into which nothing should be read.

He was offering her a brief interlude—to be enjoyed by them both while it lasted.

What was there to think about?

'It might be crazy,' she whispered, 'but what's wrong with a little craziness from time to time?'

With a moan, he pulled her towards him—brushing his mouth over hers as if he had been starved of contact for days instead of mere minutes. He felt the thunder of his heart and the urgent hardening of his groin as her soft breasts pressed against him. 'We're going to have to be discreet at all times—because my servants are all-seeing,' he warned softly. 'We must not flaunt our affair in front of them, for that would also be disrespectful to them.'

And what about me? wondered Frankie with a touch of desperation as he whispered his lips over her hair. Did her feelings matter less than those of the servants?

But she recognised that she must not waste precious time wishing for the impossible. She must enjoy what was on offer and applaud Zahid's honesty towards her. He might not be giving her the fairy-tale version of a love affair, but at least he wasn't lying to her—and surely that was showing her respect of the most fundamental kind?

'Come on,' he said, with one last, lingering kiss. 'We'd better go.'

He reached down to press the remote control and the automatic blind floated back up over the window. Frankie blinked, realising that the exceptional brightness she'd noticed before was due to the reflection of sunlight on water. Walking over to the window, she peered out and in the distance she could see the shimmer of water and the unexpected lushness of green foliage.

'Is that a river?' she questioned, in surprise.

He went to stand beside her, his hand lingering briefly on the curve of her bottom. 'Indeed it is—we call it the Jamanah river, which means "silver pearl".' He looked down and shot her a mocking look. 'I suppose you thought that all desert kingdoms were entirely without water?'

'I try to avoid generalisations like that.' Frankie screwed up her eyes as she tried to remember back to her geography lessons. 'Does it happen to have its source outside the country?'

'Bravo,' he affirmed softly. 'It's what is known as an exotic river and it flows from the neighbouring country of Sharifah.'

'Isn't that the one you had all the wars with?'

He raised his eyebrows. 'Bravo again, Francesca. How on earth did you know that?'

'My father told me, of course. He was very interested in Khayarzahian history.'

'And you've remembered it all?'

'Most of it.' She smiled to herself as they left the house and got into the car. Of course she had remembered it all! Didn't she used to collect and store up facts about Zahid like other girls used to collect Barbie dolls? Because hadn't it always fascinated her, to learn what she could about the dark sheikh she so adored and the land which was so precious to him? 'I have a very retentive memory,' she said primly.

His gaze flicked over her. 'You are a surprising woman in many ways.'

'That sounds awfully like a compliment.'

'That's because it is,' he murmured.

Frankie glowed with pleasure as he started up the engine and in that moment she couldn't ever remember feeling happier. Bathed in the warm afterglow of sex, it was easy to forget that Zahid had warned her about any long-term hopes or dreams about their relationship.

Along the way, he pointed out landmarks and the country which she'd grown up hearing so much about slowly came to life. His voice lulled her with tales of battles fought by his ancestors as they drove along the straight and dusty road through the desert, while the sun set like blood on the sand which surrounded them.

It was only when they arrived back at the palace that a subtle change occurred in him. As soon as the ornate golden gates had clanged shut behind them he went from lover to King. His expression became as remote as the distant mountains and the closeness which she'd experienced in the car all but disappeared. There was no brief pressing of flesh or brush of skin against skin as they parted. No honeyed words of affection. Instead, his tone was clipped and flat.

'I must go to speak with my advisors,' he said. 'So I'll leave you with the opportunity to rest after your afternoon in the heat. Before dinner I'll show you the diaries and where you'll be working—so that tomorrow you may begin. How does that sound?'

'That sounds fine,' she answered awkwardly, aware of the formality which had suddenly entered his voice.

And that was that. Nothing more. He was gone with not even a secret shared look or smile to remind them of the intimacy which Frankie now remembered with almost painful clarity. Was it really possible that just a couple of hours ago she'd been naked in his arms and thrilling to the brand-new experience of being made love to? Yet now he was turning away from her as if she were a stranger.

She was standing watching him walk away when Fayruz appeared, as if she had been summoned. And maybe she had, thought Frankie.

Probably all the palace machinery had started whirring the moment the sheikh had driven them into the palace forecourt.

At least there was enough time for Frankie to take extra-special care in dressing and, after she'd dismissed the servant, she looked at the array of silk clothes in her wardrobes. What had Zahid said to her, in one of those quieter moments when his lips had grazed over hers and made her shiver with longing? That her eyes were the most beautiful blue he had ever seen—bluer even than the precious mosaic stones of lapis lazuli which studded the walls of his palace?

His words made her choose a tunic and trousers in deep sapphire blue and she twisted her hair up into a knot on top of her head. It was a bold look and one she wouldn't usually have dared try—but having a man like Zahid purring compliments like that did wonders for a woman's confidence.

Fayruz came to collect her an hour before dinner and took her to where Zahid was waiting in the palace's ancient library. It was an exquisite gilded room, lined with the most beautiful books she had ever seen.

His black eyes were watchful as she walked in, but the faint curve of his smile was unmistakable, even to her. Frankie might not have been the most experienced woman on the block, but she could tell that her lover approved of her appearance. She stood before him as he dismissed Fayruz, wondering if he might quickly pull her into his arms and murmur his appreciation. But the complete absence of softness on his face made her feel nervous.

Nonetheless, her mounting nerves were suddenly subdued by the sight of the intricately inlaid box which stood on a nearby table and which he opened to reveal a neat stack of leather notebooks inside.

All thoughts and worries about her relationship with Zahid were forgotten in the light of this tangible slice of history and Frankie reached into the box with eager care, gently withdrawing the nearest volume.

The pages were a little dry but completely

intact and the flowing handwriting was—thankfully—extremely legible. Some pages were full of closely written script, while others—clearly written in times of great trouble or stress—were more bald and succinct. How her father would have loved to have seen these, she thought as her gaze skimmed over them.

After a few minutes she remembered where she was and she looked up to find Zahid watching her with a curiously intent look in his black eyes.

'I gather you like what you see,' he observed.

'I do—and I can't wait to start,' she said.

And at this, Zahid gave a rueful smile. Had he thought that she might be difficult to deal with—having had time to reflect on her sexual awakening? Imagining that she might become demanding—or start behaving inappropriately? Yet there was none of the limpet-like looks he'd anticipated—nor any soft reproachful comments that he hadn't kissed her.

No, she was currently picking up another volume of his father's work and looking as if she would like to sit down at one of the nearby tables and begin reading it from cover to cover right now! It was the first time in his life that he had ever been overlooked by someone deep in a book!

'Are you not hungry, Francesca?' he questioned drily.

Blinking, she glanced up from the diary. 'Hungry? Yes, of course I am.'

'Then perhaps you could bear to endure having dinner with me before losing yourself in my father's work.' He arched her a sardonic look as he saw her reluctantly close the book and he smiled as he saw a glimpse of the earnest schoolgirl she had once been. 'You can start transcribing first thing in the morning. Come on, let's go and eat.'

Frankie felt a sense of unreality as she walked beside him through the marble corridors. In those few moments she felt so close to him and yet so far apart. If it had been anyone but Zahid, then wouldn't they have laced fingers together and walked along, hand in hand? She now knew his body intimately and yet she had not so much as touched him since they'd returned to the palace.

But they ate in the same dining room as the previous night—which at least gave her the comfort of familiarity. Exotic platters of food were brought in and, although she ate some of the delicious morsels, Frankie was sure that she didn't do them justice. How could she, when Zahid was sitting opposite her and driving every thought from her head other than how it had felt to be made love to by him? Was it the same for him—or did one woman simply blur into another, the sexual experience forgotten once it was over?

'You're very quiet, Francesca.'

It sounded more like an observation than a question and she gave a little shrug. 'Am I?'

'In Khayarzah we have an expression— "if you give me your thought, I will give you an almond".'

'In England we say—a penny for your thoughts. Yours is much more poetic.'

'And do you like almonds?'

'I love them.'

'So?' His gaze roved over her questioningly.

'Who's Katya?' she asked suddenly.

His eyes narrowed. 'Katya?'

The question she had buried now came bubbling to the surface. 'The woman who rang that day in London, in the hotel. The one who was very sniffy with me.'

Zahid frowned. He wanted to tell her that Katya was none of her business, but something in the way she was biting her lip made him relent—and he *had* asked. 'Just a woman.'

Just? Somehow Frankie kept her expression ambiguous, wondering if she too was *just* a woman. Would someone one day refuse to let *her* speak to the sheikh when she telephoned—some smart and confident female who was currently the star in his firmament? She saw the future flash before her eyes and felt her heart sink. 'I can't think that any woman would care to hear herself described like that.'

'Okay, perhaps that wasn't the most diplomatic way to put it. She's a Russian model I had an affair with. Satisfied?'

It wasn't the best word to use in the circumstances and Frankie hated the next stupid and insecure question which seemed to blurt from her lips. 'And was she...was she very beautiful?'

He smiled at the predictably feminine response. 'No, she was as ugly as an addax.' He saw her lips wobble and lowered his voice. 'She was a model, Francesca—ergo, she was beautiful. But it's over. The affair is over—it's been over, ever since I became Sheikh. And anyway, why are you doing this, *anisah*—and why now? We're not going to spoil a beautiful affair with petty jealousies, are we?'

She shook her head, trying to ignore the dark claws of envy which were scrabbling at her heart. And hard on the heels of envy came the even more paralysing feeling of fear, even though Zahid had done nothing but speak the truth. This *was* an affair—nothing more, she knew that because he'd told her that right from the start. If she wanted more from the relationship, then not only would she be disappointed, but she would risk ruining what they already had. Somehow she dredged up a smile and hoped it looked more convincing than it felt. 'No, of course we're not.'

'Good. I am very pleased to hear it.'

So she played her part of being the polite guest rather than the jealous lover—and began asking him about the eastern mountains and the fabled leopards which lived there. And it wasn't until tiny little cups of thick, sweet coffee had been brought to the table that she slanted him a look.

'Zahid?'

'Mmm.' Steeling himself against another bout of female possessiveness, he arched his dark brows in question.

'What's an addax?' she asked.

'It's a desert antelope—famous for its ugliness.' He smiled with a sudden, comfortable indulgence. Her sense of humour and quickness of mind stimulated him, but not nearly as much as the soft thrust of her breasts. 'Go to bed, Francesca,' he commanded, in a soft and urgent tone. 'And I will join you as soon as the moon has risen.'

CHAPTER TWELVE

THE soft light of dawn crept through the shutters of her bedroom and, lazily, Frankie stirred beneath the rumpled sheet, her legs willingly trapped beneath the weight of the sheikh's hair-roughened thigh. 'Don't go,' she murmured—a request which seemed to have become a morning ritual.

'I have to go, *anisah bahiya*.' Zahid's voice was regretful, but resolute. 'Don't make this any harder for me than it already is.'

'But I thought that's what you liked...' Her fingers drifted down to tiptoe over the heavy throb of his arousal.

'Witch!' With a low growl, he grazed his mouth against her bare shoulder. 'If I leave it much later, then the servants will be up and if I am seen leaving your rooms...'

His words tailed off, but still he could not quite bring himself to move away from the warm circle of her embrace, or to still the fingers which were stroking between his thighs. How inexplicable was that? Three weeks of sharing her bed every night had proved a curiously potent addiction for a man who was usually averse to constant female companionship. Hadn't he once said to his brother that to eat dinner with the same woman two nights running was to define boredom? And hadn't Tariq given an odd kind of smile and agreed with him?

Frankie bit her lip. 'And would it be the end of the world if your servants *did* see you?'

'Of course it would. But, more importantly, it would be the end of your reputation,' he said fiercely, brushing the silken spill of dark hair away from her cheek. 'And I don't want that.'

Frankie swallowed. 'And what if I told you that I don't care about my reputation?'

'Well, you should.' Her words were the spur he needed and he got out of bed and began to pull on his robes with an economy of movement.

'Your name is respected in my country and I don't intend for that to change, Francesca. And if word got out that you were sharing my bed—that is exactly what would happen.'

She nodded as she met the determination which glittered from his black eyes and knew that to object would be pointless. 'If you say so.' She yawned as he leaned over the bed and tugged the sheet over her.

'I do. Now go back to sleep and I'll see you later.'

And with one last brief and charismatic smile, he was gone, leaving Frankie to drift in and out of sleep before it was time to get up and make her way to the library.

It was an oddly restful place to work. Scented by fragrant roses which stood on her desk and with most of the windows shuttered against the brilliant sunlight outside; she always experienced an immense feeling of peace when she walked into the vast book-lined room each morning.

As happened every day, breakfast had been laid out for her on a table overlooking the palace gardens. Mint tea, a dish of iced oranges and a selection of the very sweet pastries which the Khayarzah people loved.

She ate a little, then went to the desk and pulled out one of the diaries from an inlaid box which was hundreds of years old—something which had stopped being remarkable, because most things in the palace were ancient and beautiful. What *was* remarkable was how quickly she had settled into such a rarefied existence. Instead of being intimidated by her cloistered desert life, she had quickly settled into the exotic world of Khayarzah as if she had been born to it.

Being surrounded by priceless antiques didn't faze her—and neither did the presence of the noiseless servants who seemed to haunt the palace rooms and corridors. She'd quickly become used to luxury and comfort and taking long walks in the manicured gardens during the hours of daylight, while Zahid went about his kingly tasks.

And if she spent most of the day alone—she made up for it in the evenings, when Zahid would usually join her for dinner. Afterwards, they would sometimes sit playing cards—just as they'd done all those years ago. Only these days he no longer let her beat him. These days she had to really *try* in order to win. And that wasn't terribly easy when sexual tension seemed to sizzle in the air around them.

Sometimes, there were nights when Zahid needed to attend some glittering social function and then she would read up on the history of Khayarzah—curled up on an embroidered sofa in one of the less intimidating salons.

'You don't mind being left alone?' he'd asked her one evening, appearing in the doorway in shimmering robes of muted silver.

Of course she'd minded but, recognising that complaining wasn't going to get her anywhere, she'd shaken her head. What choice did she have but to put up with it? It simply wouldn't be done for him to turn up at a formal function with a foreign woman by his side. 'Not at all. I'm used to my own company.' And she had seen him nod his dark head with satisfaction, pleased with her reply.

But by night it was a different story. When the moon was high in the star-spangled Khayarzahian sky, he would come to her room and silently ravish her in the warm, scented darkness. Heart hammering like a piston, she would lie awake waiting for him—naked and eager beneath Egyptian cotton sheets as she heard the soft whisper of his clothes sliding to the marble floor. And then he would join her on the bed, his hard, virile body hot and hungry, his kisses full of urgent passion. He would make love to her for most of the night until their bodies were exhausted—slipping away only when the milky light of dawn turned the sky a pale apricot colour.

Leaving Frankie to drift off into a dazed sleep. So that sometimes when she opened her heavy eyes in the morning she would wonder whether perhaps she had dreamt the whole thing.

The diaries helped. Having a legitimate reason to be in the palace gave her a sense of purpose and stopped her thinking about what she would do when the affair was over. Because the thought of leaving Zahid was too painful to contemplate. She couldn't imagine it—didn't want to imagine it. Much better to remember what it felt like when he made love to her, when his clever tongue licked all the way up her thigh and then…then…

Frankie closed her eyes with erotic recall. Memories of his love-making always overwhelmed her, but she was aware of something else happening. Something dangerous, deep inside her heart. Because in tandem with the physical flowering of her body had come a new and unwanted emotion and somewhere along the way she had fallen in love with the hawk-faced king. The caring friendship she'd always felt had grown into something much bigger and infinitely more powerful.

She loved him.

Would he be horrified if he knew how she felt?

Frankie stared down at the diary which lay open on the desk but none of the words registered. Of course he would! He'd be more than horrified. Love wasn't on the agenda and it never had been. He'd told her that in no uncertain terms. This was all about sex—great sex, it was true—but nothing more than that.

'I'm not paying you to sit there daydreaming, you know.'

A mocking voice broke into her thoughts as Zahid walked into the library and Frankie looked at him, her heart melting as she stared into the black glitter of his eyes.

'Sometimes I can't help daydreaming,' she defended softly.

'About?'

About the way you hold me when your body is deep inside mine. About the way you kiss me when it's all over. About how much I'd love to stay here, by your side, for ever. But such words could never be uttered. They were forbidden— just as driving was forbidden and showing affection towards each other in public. And being found in bed together. So, with an effort, Frankie scrambled together her thoughts and gestured towards the open leather journal in front of her.

'About your father's diary—it's a fascinating document.'

'In terms of content, you mean—or just generally?'

'Both. A diary is better than an autobiography, don't you think? Much more personal.'

Zahid nodded. 'An intimate glimpse into someone's life, you mean—as well as their thoughts?'

'Well, yes.' She could understand why nobody outside the family had ever seen them before— for they were almost painful in their intimacy. 'Things I already knew, I now see differently. It makes me realise how difficult it must have been for you all, with the war and everything.' She hesitated, wondering whether this was a forbidden subject, too. Perhaps it was, since they had never talked about it. 'And then, when your mother became ill.'

Zahid's face tightened with a sense of inevitability. But maybe he should have realised that by giving her access to his father's work, he would be opening up a part of himself which he had always kept locked away. For a man so fiercely self-contained, it was a disturbing thought that she was delving beneath the surface of his life and seeing into the hidden depths. But this was Francesca, he reminded himself—a woman who knew him almost better than anyone. He could say things to her that he wouldn't for a moment contemplate saying to another.

'It wasn't easy—especially as my father found it difficult to juggle everything,' he admitted. 'As well as my mother's illness, he was busy helping my uncle repair the country after so many years of war. And there was too much going on for him to devote much time to his two lively young sons. It was one of the reasons why Tariq and I spent some of our education in boarding school in England—something which gave us a taste of a very different life. It was far worse for Tariq of course, for he was younger and he…he never really got a chance to know our mother.'

He'd never been quite so forthcoming before and Frankie hesitated, afraid that more questions might make the familiar shutters come down. Yet her need to know overrode her natural caution.

'It must have been a terrible shock for you, when your uncle died.'

There was silence for a moment. Nobody had ever asked him that. His feelings had never been discussed—for his accession to the throne had been a given. And mightn't the natural doubts he had experienced at the time have been interpreted as weakness if he had dared express them?

'It was an utter shock,' answered Zahid simply. 'But the worse thing was that *his* son—the rightful heir—was with him at the time. They should never have been allowed to travel together— and normally they wouldn't have done. But the light over the mountains was fading, there was only one available plane and the decision was made that they should go on the same flight.' He paused. 'And in that split second, their destiny was decided.'

Zahid's face hardened as he remembered the broken pieces of the aeroplane lying in pieces on the ground. His own father had not long died and then he had to cope with these two new deaths in

quick succession—followed by a sombre crowning as he was made King. He had never wanted
to be King and yet he could not have admitted that to anyone. And in time, he had grown
into the role which he had at first resented. A
role which still carried with it strict boundaries,
which he must ensure he never forgot.

'I'm so sorry,' said Frankie.

He looked at her, her words breaking him from
his reverie and bringing him back to the present.
Reminding him with an unwelcome shock of
just how very un-kinglike his current mode of
behaviour was. He had taken his oldest friend as
his lover and at times he had expressed concern
about what he was doing to her reputation. But
what of his?

Wouldn't his people be appalled if they realised
that he was cavorting with a western woman
within the palace walls? And could he really
hold himself up as some kind of national moral
guardian, when he was rejecting all the values
which the Khayarzahian people held so dear?

His eyes were drawn to her face—to cheeks

the colour of the palest rose and eyes which were bluer than the desert sky. He found himself remembering how sweetly her arms opened for him every night, and how eagerly her body welcomed him. All the pleasures of the body he had taught her, she had embraced with enthusiasm. How he would like this affair to continue—to carry on, just as they were.

But he was not being fair—not to her, and not to his people. Unlike his brother Tariq, he was not a gambling man—but he knew enough about odds and probability to realise that if they continued being lovers, then eventually they would be found out. And then what?

His mouth hardened. He needed to talk to her—and not in bed where the distractions of her delicious body might cause his resolve to waver. Nor here, where the unseen servants might read their body language even if they could not understand their words. Somewhere away from the palace—a place which she had previously talked about—he needed to say to Francesca the words she deserved to hear.

He glanced at her from between narrowed eyes. 'Today, my diary is almost empty and I had been intending to catch up on some paperwork. But instead, I shall order the kitchens to make us up a picnic and we will go out somewhere for lunch. Somewhere quiet. Would you like that, Francesca?'

Startled by the unexpected and unfamiliar invitation, Frankie felt the leap of excitement. 'I'd absolutely love it.'

'Good. Then it shall be done. We shall be alone.'

'You mean…your bodyguards won't be there?' she ventured, in surprise.

'They will keep their distance,' he said softly. 'Now let me go and organise it.'

They set off just before midday and Zahid drove the big Jeep through the stark terrain. But Frankie was too excited to concentrate on the journey—even when he said that they were heading for the foothills of the eastern mountains. Her father had once told her that it was one of the most beautiful places on earth—and that you could know true peace in a place like that. Yet peaceful was the last thing she felt as she glanced at the sheikh's hard, hawklike profile and the faint shading of new growth at his jaw.

She was aware of an undeniable feeling of excitement building and building inside her—and she couldn't quite work out why. Was it because this was the first time they had done anything remotely normal—like a *real* couple? And did such an action mark a new openness in Zahid's behaviour towards her?

'See up there is the mighty *Nouf* mountain,' Zahid said softly as they drove towards the massive peak which dominated the landscape. 'Where the mountain's shadow and the rare waters which trickle from the top make fertile the land beneath. Where the peaks look purple in the sunset and where falcons soar in the thermal winds.'

'Oh, but it's beautiful,' she breathed.

Her genuine awe made his heart ache as he realised that what he was about to do was not going to be easy. Zahid stopped the car and turned to her. 'Come, we will take our food and our drink and sit in the shade of the rocks awhile—for you must be thirsty.'

Her throat *was* dry, but the sweet, iced melon juice he poured into one of the silver cups which they unpacked from the picnic basket quickly refreshed her. Zahid drank deeply and then put his own cup down, removed hers from her suddenly nerveless fingers and took both her hands in his own.

'I need to talk to you,' he said.

Something in the tone of his voice unsettled her. 'That sounds ominous,' she joked, but a little shiver of apprehension began to whisper its way down her spine.

'Does it?'

'Yes.' She watched as his face became shuttered and her sense of trepidation mounted. 'Why did you bring me here today, Zahid?'

He traced a butterfly circle on her palm with the tip of his finger and then looked up at her. 'We need to talk about the future.'

She felt the flare of both hope and fear in the

sudden leap of her heart as she stared into the dark gleam of his eyes. 'D-do we? What about it?'

'None of this has been as I planned it,' he said suddenly. 'I never planned—foolishly, as it happens—to take you as my lover. I told you back in England that I thought I could resist you—but now it seems that was an arrogant and unrealistic assessment of my own will power.'

In spite of all the intimacies they had known in bed, she found herself blushing at his growled admission. 'Yes.'

'Of course, if you had told me that you were a virgin, then I *would* have resisted you.' There was a heartbeat of a pause. 'But you didn't tell me, did you?'

'No.' Frankie bit her lip—because now she could definitely hear *reprimand* in his voice. 'No, I didn't.'

'And once I'd possessed you, it was too late,' he added. 'For by then I was ensnared.'

She looked at him, unsure of how to respond.

Was that supposed to be a compliment, or some kind of territorial boast? 'Ensnared?' she echoed.

'You don't like the word? Would captivated suit you better?'

She nodded, still not certain where any of this was leading. 'Maybe.'

He gave a short laugh. How refreshingly honest she was. And how beautiful. All that sweet promise which could never be his. Soon, her delicious, scented body would no longer grace his sheets at night. With any other woman, it would have been a simple matter to dispatch her—but surely Francesca deserved the truth. 'Maybe you want me to say that I love you?' he questioned quietly. 'As I think you love me.'

She felt her stomach twist itself up into little knots because words of love weren't usually accompanied by a heavy weariness of the voice. And there was something dark written on his face which was filling her with foreboding. 'Not if it isn't true.'

'Because I do,' he said, as if she hadn't spoken. 'You see, I do love you, my *anisah bahiya*.'

Her lips were trembling so much that her stammered response was barely audible. 'You *d-do*?'

Grimly, he nodded his dark head. 'Yes. Unfortunately, I do. And it's because I love you that I'm afraid I have to send you away from here.'

CHAPTER THIRTEEN

THERE was a dense and heavy silence while Frankie's emotions took a trip on some demented roller coaster, which rocked her to the core. 'You say you love me, yet you're sending me away?' she whispered.

Zahid nodded, determined that the sapphire swim of her eyes would not sway him. Didn't she realise what such an admission of love had cost him? 'I have to.'

Perhaps pride should have stopped her from interrogating him—but what price pride when her whole future lay at stake? 'I don't understand.'

'You will if you think about it, Francesca. The longer you're here—the more I risk compromising your reputation. You say you don't care about such a thing, but I do. More than that, we both risk getting deeper and deeper into a relationship which has no future—not now and not ever. I must marry a woman from my own country,' he said bitterly. 'I told you that at the very beginning and nothing has changed.' Except that he had behaved like an impetuous and thoughtless fool and they would now both pay the price for that behaviour. 'I must take a wife—or two—maybe even three.'

The bizarre conversation they were having now took on an even more surreal aspect. 'Three?' she echoed as she snatched her hand away from his. 'Three wives?'

He met the disbelieving blue blaze in her eyes. 'I am allowed four by law, although I doubt whether I—'

'Zahid, *please*!' Frankie interrupted and her sorrow was replaced by an indignant kind of fury. 'Please don't stand there and make out that we have no future because you're following some kind of *moral* code—and then add that you're going to take what amounts to almost an entire football team of wives!'

He guessed that now was not the time to point

out that her numbers were out by about seven. He reached towards her again but she shook her head, stepping back from him as if he were contaminated. 'Francesca—'

'Don't touch me.' She was aware that her eyes were swimming with tears but she didn't care. 'Why did you bring me here today—so far from the palace? Why didn't you just tell me back there?'

Because he had wanted to avoid someone overhearing exactly the kind of scene they were having now. The kind of scene he'd never had with a woman—because no woman had ever got this close to him before. And if he was being honest, hadn't he thought that he might win her round with kisses and soft caresses? Hadn't there been a stupid, unrealistic part of him which had hoped that she might agree to continue their affair back in England? With him visiting her as often as he could—showering her with gifts and luxuries as if that might in some way compensate for his absence?

But he could not do that, he recognised. Not

to Francesca. He could not offer her so little because that would devalue the kind of person she was. And it would sully what they had both shared.

'I'm sorry,' he said simply.

'Don't—*don't* apologise,' she said fiercely. 'I'm not some kind of *victim*, Zahid. So will you please take me back to the palace now? And then I'd like to return immediately to England.'

Zahid tensed up, for he was unused to anyone laying down furious demands like this—yet even he could see that she had a right to be angry. But surely they needn't part on terms of such bitterness. Couldn't they end this affair the same way they'd started it—consumed and comforted by the act of love?

'You can, of course, return to England,' he said smoothly. 'And my jet will take you there, but I'm afraid that we'll have to go via Morocco.'

Suspiciously, she stared at him. *'Morocco?'*

'Indeed,' he said, with a shrug. 'I have a friend named Raffaele de Ferretti—we go back a long way. I've arranged to spend the weekend with him in Marrakech and he's expecting us. We will leave tonight.'

'Do I have any choice?'

'I'm afraid not.'

Zahid began to pick up the picnic hamper. He had planned to surprise her with a trip to the exotic north African city. But that had been when he'd thought their affair could continue without consequence. Before he'd been forced to acknowledge that something between them had changed…

But pride would not let him turn up without the woman he had told his Italian friend about on the phone last week. And surely she wouldn't be able to resist him, when the two of them were sharing a luxury suite in a romantic *riad*?

The journey back to the palace was completed in silence and when they arrived Frankie went straight to her suite of rooms to pack. At least she wouldn't have to wear any more of these stupid tunics with their matching narrow-legged trousers, she thought—until she sat down on the edge of the low divan and bit her lip.

She *liked* wearing those silky-soft tunics—whose very qualities of concealment meant that a woman could feel curiously liberated when she had them on. It made quite a change not to have to worry about whether your bottom looked big or whether you were showing too much cleavage, or sitting in a ladylike fashion.

She was still sitting there, gulping down the threat of tears, when a perplexed-looking Fayruz arrived to tell her that the car was waiting to take them to the airport and the servant turned to Frankie with a troubled face.

'You are leaving Khayarzah?' she questioned.

'I'm afraid that I've got to go back to England, Fayruz.'

'But...'

The girl's words tailed off miserably but Frankie knew it was inappropriate to ask what was troubling her. She *knew* exactly what was troubling her, because she was experiencing similar feelings of misery herself. Fayruz didn't want her to go—and Frankie herself didn't *want* to go. But she had to. The dream she had always nurtured had come true and Zahid had told her that he loved her. And hot on the heels of that wonderful revelation had been her banishment from his kingdom. How on earth could she tell the young servant *that* without compromising the king and breaking down in floods of tears?

So she embraced Fayruz and said goodbye, promising to send her an English dictionary when she arrived home. And then, with one last look round, she went out to the car, where Zahid was seated in the front, in the passenger seat.

He gave her only the most cursory of greetings and spoke to his driver all the way to the airport. And even though that didn't surprise her, it didn't stop her from hurting.

Even on the lavishly appointed Gulfstream jet, Zahid sat working at a table some distance away from her and Frankie wondered if he was going to ignore her the entire weekend. How was he going to introduce her to his Italian friend? *Hello, this is Francesca—you're very welcome to speak to her, but I'm afraid I won't be doing the same.*

The plane landed in the warm spiciness of the Moroccan night, where the indigo sky was peppered with bright stars. Immediately, they were whisked through passport control—but when Frankie raised her head after putting away her passport with trembling fingers, it was to see Zahid subjecting her to a narrow-eyed look.

'You've never been to Morocco before, have you?' he questioned.

She shook her head. 'Never.'

Another wave of unwanted guilt washed over him at the sight of her pinched and unhappy face. Had he done that to her? Brought her out here to heal the pain of her broken engagement and then ended up hurting her much more? And himself, he realised. He was hurting with a pain he'd never experienced. 'It's a very beautiful city,' he said heavily. 'As you will discover for yourself in the morning.'

Frankie tried to concentrate on the loveliness of her surroundings and the pleasure of this brand-new experience as their car drove them through the walls of the ancient city.

The place where they were staying was stunning. It was situated right in the very heart of Marrakech and not far from the hustle and bustle of the lively market they called the Medina. Here, in their *riad* was a perfect blend of Middle Eastern opulence with every modern convenience you could ever want. There was a massage room and sauna—as well as a floodlit courtyard swimming pool, which glittered gold and turquoise in the moonlight.

And a sumptuous suite with an enormous, low bed.

She stood looking down at it as if it had been covered with a writhing nest of vipers and then Zahid turned to look at her.

'We could have our first full night together,' he said softly.

'We could—but it isn't going to happen.'

'Francesca—'

'I can't,' she said simply, because she was only just about holding it together as it was. Imagine if he kissed her—if she let him enter her body again after everything which had happened? 'I'll sleep on that divan over there.'

'You don't have to.'

'Yes, I do. You're much too tall to be comfortable on it.'

'Very well.' His voice was cool, remote. 'If that is what you wish.'

'It is.'

But that didn't stop her heart from aching as she lay sleepless in the small hours while Zahid slept, his hawklike face looking oddly soft in sleep as it lay, pillowed by his forearm.

Raffaele arrived next day with his fiancée— but Francesca was too exhausted from lack of sleep to meet them until dinner. She spent most of the day reading while Zahid worked and they communicated with a cool politeness she found far more distressing than the row they'd had in the desert.

Unfortunately, she fell asleep while she was supposed to be getting ready—and so by the time she stumbled downstairs the others were already assembled on the rooftop terrace, drinking from heavy red goblets and nibbling at pistachios.

Zahid's face was a mask of disapproval as she walked onto the terrace.

'You are late,' he said.

Frankie shot him a reproving glance. 'Zahid, aren't you going to introduce us?'

Zahid made no attempt to hide his frown. Was there no *end* to her stubborn behaviour? he asked himself angrily. She had refused to share a bed with him and now she was *late*. 'This is Raffaele de Ferretti, a business colleague, and this is his fiancée, Natasha—'

'Phillips,' butted in the woman with silky-looking hair and a rather anxious look on her face.

'This is Francesca,' Zahid said.

'Hello,' said Francesca, and smiled—even though it seemed to take a monumental effort to do so. Just as it took an even bigger effort to get through the meal without breaking down. Especially since Raffaele and his fiancée were clearly on some sort of high. The air was heavy with the sexual tension which seemed to flow between them and which made even more mockery of Frankie's own life and her situation with Zahid.

By the time the evening was over and she and the sheikh were back in their suite, she stared at him as he closed the door.

'Count me out for any further encounters like that,' she said quietly.

'We have a whole weekend to get through,' he objected coldly.

'And I'll spend it in the suite.'

'You can't do that.'

'Oh, but I can.' She stared at him, defying him to challenge her. 'I can do exactly as I please, Zahid. I'm a free agent, aren't I?'

And that was that. Frankie stayed in their suite for the rest of their stay and Zahid presumably made excuses for her absence—because as soon as was decently possible the whole miserable visit was cut short.

'Get your clothes packed,' he bit out. 'We're leaving.'

'What, now?'

'Yes. Now.'

The journey to the airfield was spent with Frankie biting on her lip and trying desperately hard not to break down in front of him. But it wasn't easy. It felt as if someone had punched a hole in her heart and left it aching and empty. When would this feeling go? she wondered distractedly. How long did it take for love to die?

Their limousine drew up onto the tarmac and she was wondering how they would endure the long flight ahead when, to her surprise and consternation, Zahid said goodbye.

'Goodbye?' Sheer panic made all the blood drain from her face. 'But I thought…I mean, aren't you supposed to be flying to London with me?'

'I was,' he corrected and he looked deep into her eyes, feeling the painful twist of his heart as he registered the whiteness of her face. 'But I've changed my mind. I don't think we need endure any more of this painful charade.'

'Zahid—'

'No, Francesca. Maybe it's best this way. Let's

just try and retain some of the good memories, shall we?' he questioned bitterly—because much more of this and he would do something unforgivable. Like break down in front of her. And what good would that do? It wouldn't actually *change* anything.

The aircraft steps were lowered and Frankie was suddenly stricken by an overwhelming sense of fear as she stared up into the harshness of his shadowed features. He was going! He was going and she might realistically never see him again. In all the years which lay ahead, this might be her last glance at his beloved face. Because she realised something else, too. That their friendship of so many years had been irreparably shattered by the end of their affair. And that hurt almost more than anything else.

She took a tentative step forward, not knowing what she was going to say but knowing that she needed to touch him one last time. Just to feel the warm brush of his skin…

'Zahid?'

'What?' He could read the unbearable sadness

in her eyes but he kept his distance, knowing that if they touched he would be lost. Instead, he shrugged. 'What can I say, other than that I'm sorry?'

'S-sorry?' The lump in her throat was threatening to choke her. 'You mean you regret what has happened?'

Zahid's mouth hardened. Yes, of course he regretted it—because their affair had given him a taste of a paradise he sensed he would never know again. But the tentative buckling of her rose-pink lips made something inside him melt and revise his opinion. For how could he regret something which had given him so much joy, and fulfilment? He shook his head. 'Of course I don't regret it,' he whispered. 'I'm just sorry that I can't offer you anything more.'

'Zahid.' Her eyes were now brimming with tears and she wanted to blurt out that she would be satisfied with whatever he *was* able to offer her. That she would be contented to be his London mistress if she could continue being his lover—no matter how short and how snatched his visits might be. But Frankie knew that was not the answer. Wouldn't she become increasingly dissatisfied if her sheikh tossed out ever smaller scraps of his time, until there was no respect or love left between them? Far better to part now, while the memories were sweet—no matter how much it hurt to do so.

'Zahid,' she said again, knowing that there was something she needed to tell him—even if it meant that she made herself even more vulnerable in the process.

'What?' he questioned grimly.

Say it, she told herself fiercely. Say it so that he will never be in any doubt of the truth. 'I just want you to know that I love you, my darling. I love you so much.'

Zahid flinched, for it was like having his heart pierced with the sharpest of all swords. 'I know you do,' he answered softly. 'Just as I love you. Now go. Go before…'

She nodded as she heard the sudden break in his voice. 'Goodbye, my love,' she whispered.

'Goodbye, Francesca.' He turned on his heel

and began to walk away from her, scarcely aware of the aide who appeared and informed him that a jet was being fuelled for his return journey to Khayarzah. All Zahid registered was the sight of Francesca's plane as it took off into the star-filled Moroccan sky and he stood watching it until it had disappeared.

And only then did he board his own plane with a heavy heart—before going straight to the washroom and locking the door.

For there were very few places where a king could cry.

CHAPTER FOURTEEN

'WILL there be anything else, Your Royal Highness?'

Zahid stared at the aide who was standing in front of him with a questioning look on his face and realised that he had been lost in thought. That he had sat through an entire meeting to discuss the opening of the new horse-racing track and that most of it had gone right over his head. Again.

This could not go on.

Flexing and then unflexing his long fingers, he shook his head. 'No, there will be nothing else.'

'We still need to discuss the opening ceremony,' reminded the aide delicately.

'I said, not *now*,' snapped Zahid and could not miss the unmistakable glance which shimmered between his two closest advisors. They were wondering what the hell was the matter with him lately. Why he seemed to have the attention span of a fly and why nothing seemed to bring him pleasure.

Hadn't he been wondering the same thing himself?

Abruptly, he stood up—a movement which brought the assembled group leaping to their feet. And bitterly Zahid recognised that it was a sign of ignorance if you failed to acknowledge what, deep down, you knew to be the truth. Because the reason for his discontentment and heavy heart was as clear as the bright Khayarzah morning.

He missed Francesca.

He missed her in a way that he imagined a man might miss his limb if it had been torn from his body, leaving him shocked and bleeding.

Hadn't he thought that it would be easy? That by doing the right thing by his country, he would soon forget about the sapphire-eyed friend who had burrowed her way into his heart? Somehow, he had imagined that duty would bring some kind of consolation, in the form of some sort of peace of mind. But duty had so far failed to deliver.

Hadn't he done everything he could to stop himself from thinking about her? Thrown himself into every task with a fervour which had astonished his palace staff—as if sheer hard work might provide him with some kind of sanctuary? And when that had failed, hadn't he taken his horse and ridden him in the cool of the desert evening—ridden him harder than he could remember riding for years? But physical exhaustion, sweat and dust had done little to alleviate the terrible emptiness which filled him like a vacuum.

The other night, his brother Tariq had even called from London, on some flimsy pretext—but Zahid had known immediately that the subtext was to enquire how he was. Did that mean that word had got back to him that the ruling sheikh was out of sorts? And did such rumours not threaten to bring instability to Khayarzah? Maybe the ridiculous irony of the whole sorry mess was that the right thing might turn out to be the *wrong* thing?

His face darkened with rage, and the thought that he could be harming his beloved country was enough to spur him into immediate action. Gathering together his aides, he told them that he was making a short trip to England—and by the following day his Gulfstream jet was touching down outside London.

The black car he always used when visiting the country had been brought to the airfield and, after briefing his bodyguards, he set off on the familiar roads towards Francesca's Surrey home, just as dusk was descending.

Fairy lights twinkled in garden bushes and blazed from the windows of the houses he passed—so that the usually subdued suburban roads seemed to resemble some sort of carnival. And then he remembered that it was December, and Christmas—when the whole of the western world seemed to come alight with colour and joy. He glanced down at his watch to read the date.

December twenty-fourth.

The night before Christmas.

Zahid narrowed his eyes. Wasn't that a big deal? When stockings were hung at the ends of beds and carols sung in churches, and, for some European cultures, a feast of fish eaten at midnight? Wasn't this the time when families came together to celebrate and to remember? Close units united against the outside world...

For a moment, a terrible wave of longing washed over him and he almost turned back— until he remembered that Francesca had no family with which to sit around a festive table. She was as alone as he was...

But as he turned into the familiar driveway and flashed at the following bodyguards to instruct them to lay in wait by the gates he almost collided with a saloon car which was roaring in the opposite direction. And in the driving seat, his face tight with fury, was Simon Forrester.

Zahid had only met Francesca's fiancé once— but once had been enough to remember the sullen curl of his mouth and the handsome, pampered face. He felt something like a dark rage twisting in his gut.

What the hell was he doing here?

Screeching to a halt in front of the house in a spray of gravel, Zahid leapt out of the car and strode up to the house—hammering on the door until it opened and a startled looking Francesca stood blinking up at him. He saw the colour drain from her face and the tip of her tongue dart out to moisten those petal lips. She looked as if she had just seen a ghost. Or was that guilt he read on her face? he thought grimly.

'What the hell was that creep Forrester doing here?' he demanded.

Frankie's senses were in disarray, her heart beating so loudly that it threatened to deafen her as she stared at her Sheikh lover. *Ex*-lover, she reminded herself bitterly. And ex for a good reason. Because a man who wanted four wives and who would always be a desert sheikh in the most traditional sense of the word was not the right kind of man for her. She just had to keep convincing herself of that.

She swallowed. 'You can't just turn up out of the blue, sounding like some B-rated detective, Zahid!' she protested. 'Why...why are you here?'

'Why do you think I'm here?' His voice was unsteady as he stared at her and noticed the deep shadows beneath her cheekbones—and how loose the pale sweater and jeans looked on her narrow frame. 'To talk to you.'

Frankie's heart gave a flare of hope which she did her best to ignore as she reminded herself of how many nights she had wept into her pillow over him. 'You mean you want to interrogate me about who I'm seeing?' she demanded.

'So you *are* seeing him?'

'Oh, for heaven's *sake*!' A ragged sigh of inevitability escaped from her lips. She knew that she was going to listen to what he had come to say— for how could she turn him away? But one thing was for sure. She was going to be strong. Very strong. The last time he had seen her she had been on the brink of tears and now she needed to show him that she could cope perfectly well without him. 'You'd better come in.'

He noticed that she didn't offer him tea and she didn't take him to the kitchen with its warm range and faded comfort either. He followed her into the room where he'd carried her on the day she'd discovered her fiancé's duplicity, and once there she looked at him with a proud expression on her face.

And Zahid felt the sudden unfamiliar shimmering of apprehension. Surely there could only be one reason why she could look so secure?

'You are back with him?' he questioned, unprepared for the savage lurch of his heart.

'Of course I'm not *back* with him! Do you really think I am as shallow as that?'

'Then why is he here?'

She could see the angry fire spitting from eyes which were narrowed into onyx chips. She thought that if Zahid were suddenly called upon to take a part in the pantomime which was playing to packed houses in the local theatre, he would have made a superb fire-breathing dragon.

'Actually, he was here on a mission,' she said.

'He'd heard I was back from Khayarzah and he came asking for his engagement ring back.'

Zahid remembered the Englishman's furious expression as their cars had passed at the end of the drive and, instinctively, he glanced at her bare hand. 'Which you gave to him?'

'Well, I would have done, if only I could find the damned thing.' She read the question in his eyes and shrugged. 'I seem to have mislaid it somewhere around the house. At any rate, it's missing, and when I told Simon he demanded that I give him the twenty-five thousand pounds he'd paid for it.'

Zahid stilled. 'But you didn't, did you?'

'Are you kidding?' Frankie gave a short laugh. 'Even if I *had* that kind of money—there's no way I would have given it to him. I asked him to produce a receipt which he should have had for a sum that big but, of course, he couldn't—because the ring's a fake.' She met his eyes with a challenging look. 'Something which you knew all along, didn't you, Zahid?' she questioned quietly.

Unexpectedly, Zahid's mouth quirked into a

wry half-smile. How she surprised him. Time after time, Francesca O'Hara pulled something different out of the bag to remind him of how complex and remarkable she really was. 'I didn't *know*, not for sure—fakes are increasingly sophisticated these days, and only an expert can truly tell the difference. But looking at his behaviour towards you, he didn't give the impression of someone who would spend thousands of pounds on a ring.' His eyes narrowed. 'What did he say?'

'Oh, he blustered. Made threats—all of which I ignored.' And it had felt good to stand up to him, Frankie realised—something which she would never have done in the past. She stared at Zahid, realising how much she had grown, and how much she had learned by being his mistress. She'd discovered that once you'd had the courage to tell a powerful king a few home truths, then standing up to a blustering small-town estate agent had been simple. 'I told him to go ahead and sue me!'

'Bravo, Francesca,' he said softly.

The gentling of his voice was her undoing. No longer able to seek refuge in the subject of a worthless ring, Frankie looked at him, some of her bravado leaving her. If he was here with some valiant attempt to show that they still could be friends, well, she didn't want to hear it. She wasn't ready to be friends with him again. Not yet. Maybe not ever… Swallowing down the ever-present hint of heartache, she looked at him. 'So what really brings you here today, Zahid?'

Sapphire light gleamed from her eyes and Zahid found himself lost for words as their gazes clashed. He realised that he could growl at her. He could pull her into his arms and kiss away that fierce look on her face. He could promise her a king's ransom in the truest sense of the world.

But some bone-deep instinct told him that none of these would work, not in the long run—because Frankie was not a woman to be bargained with or bought, or seduced into his way of thinking. He wanted her in every sense, he realised—but most of all he wanted her to come to him *of her own free will*.

He said the words which once would have sounded like an admission of weakness. 'I've missed you.'

I've missed you, too. I've missed you more than I thought it was ever possible to miss someone. But acknowledging that wasn't going to change anything, was it? He was still unable to offer her any kind of future. Forcing herself to ignore the plaintive tug of her heart, Frankie shrugged.

His face darkened when she made no response and so, reluctantly, he was forced to elaborate—his words a growled statement. 'And I can't seem to stop thinking about you.'

Still she said nothing, nor gave any indication that she liked what he said—and suddenly Zahid realised the true meaning of the word courage. In his youth, during a spell in the Khayarzahian army he had fought bloody battles and known real hunger. He had slept beneath the stars in the most inhospitable parts of the desert, untroubled by the threat of the scorpions and snakes nearby. His physical daring was admired and feared in equal measures by his compatriots, and it was said that there was no more intrepid rider than Zahid Al Hakam.

But did he have the kind of courage to tell this woman what lay almost buried at the bottom of his heart? An admission which would make her realise the immense power she had over him?

'I told you that I loved you, Francesca,' he said. 'But that I couldn't marry you. And I guess I thought that I would get over it. You know, like a head-cold, or a broken leg. But the truth is that I haven't. If anything the feeling is worse—'

'*Worse?*'

Had that been the wrong word? he wondered dazedly. Had he implied that it was somehow a *bad* feeling, this love he felt for her? But it *was* a bad feeling, he recognised. A negative and destructive one—if this love was not allowed the room and the right to grow and mature.

'My life is empty without you,' he admitted. 'I gave you up because I wanted to fulfil all the demands made of me by my country. But I now know I cannot rule without the woman I love beside me. And that is the truth.'

That did get a reaction. Francesca shook her head and bit down on her lips, like someone who had just witnessed something distressing.

'Please don't, Zahid,' she whispered, her voice now perilously close to tears, despite her determination not to break down in front of him. 'That's not the point. You *may* love me—as you must know that I love you—and that's rather wonderful. Because love is. But it doesn't actually *change* anything, does it? And I can't be your wife because I'm not Khayarzah born—'

'I will have the law changed,' he said arrogantly. 'For I am the king and I can.'

She carried on as if he hadn't interrupted her. 'And I certainly can't contemplate sharing you with three other wives—'

'But you will be my *only* wife!' he declared savagely. 'For I have decided to renounce all my rights to take any others—this is what I have come here today to tell you! I will not rest until you are my wife. *My only wife.*'

Frankie could see what that statement had cost him, just as she could see the passion which had animated his dark and hawklike features. And even though her heart swelled up with an overwhelming wave of love and longing, she forced herself not to be swayed by his emotional declaration. Because short-term gain would inevitably produce long-term pain.

'It won't work.'

'Why not?'

'Because it's not enough, my darling,' she said, her voice soft and trembling with emotion.

His eyes narrowed. 'What do you mean, it's not enough?'

She swallowed. 'I can't...I can't live in a country where I'm not even allowed to drive or women are discouraged from going to university.'

There was a long and disbelieving silence. 'You come to me with no dowry—and I accept that without a murmur,' he declared. 'I renounce my rights to other women and tell you that you will be my only love—and *still* it is not enough? You are now asking me to change yet more laws of my land before you will consent to be my bride?'

She shook her head. 'Of course I'm not. This

isn't some kind of bidding war we're engaged
in! I'm not asking you or telling you to do anything—just explaining what I must be true to.
And I must be true to myself. You've made me
grow as a woman and as a person, Zahid. I am
no longer the innocent and naïve person who was
duped by Simon. And while I thank you for that
from the bottom of my heart—it is also something of a double-edged sword.' She sucked in
a deep breath. 'Because I can't now take a step
backwards. I can't do something which I think
is fundamentally unsound—and I can't live in
a country where women are second-class citi-
zens—no matter how much I love the man who
leads that country.'

Silence hung heavily in the air as Zahid said
nothing—for her words were too important to
be answered without him giving them careful
consideration. He turned and walked over to
the French windows which overlooked the big
garden which had so fascinated him during his
growing up. Such a green and lush oasis it had
always seemed to the boy from the desert. But

there was no green today. Everything looked black and white. The frost was thick and the bare branches of the big trees looked as if they had been daubed in bleached and glittering brush strokes.

He sighed. Surely everything *was* black and white—in more ways than one? Francesca had had the temerity to tell him what he knew was frequently on the minds of many—sentiments which had been growing stronger over the years. For hadn't he read the outraged leader pages in western newspapers—and once, in New York, come face to face with some banner-waving women who had been demanding equal rights for women?

Was he not guilty of hypocrisy—taking western lovers as and when it suited him, while keeping the females of Khayarzah shackled in the past? Yet there was a solution. And Francesca had made him see that such a solution would be possible. It would be difficult to change, and painful, too—but change was part of life and to try to stop that was as futile as King Canute trying to turn back the tide.

And did he have a choice? Could he bear the thought of going through his own life without his strong and sapphire-eyed Francesca beside him? The woman who had shown him what it meant to love?

He turned to face her. 'The legislation cannot be changed overnight,' he warned.

She heard the promise in his voice and knew that she had to meet it halfway. 'But I know that you wouldn't drag your feet, just for the sake of it.'

Zahid smiled. There! She had done it again. By voicing her confidence and her trust in him, she had made it morally impossible for him to do anything but obey her!

'I will drag my feet on nothing,' he growled. 'Especially not this.' And he strode across the room and pulled her into his arms, his eyes blazing as he looked down at her. 'I love you, Francesca O'Hara—you and only you, for the rest of my life. You are the only woman I have ever truly wanted and ever shall want. You have captured my heart and my soul and my body—and I am asking you once again, will you marry me?'

'Oh, yes, my darling,' she said softly, her fingertips moving to trace the outline of his sensual mouth. 'Yes and yes, and a thousand times yes.'

For a moment Zahid just enjoyed the unfamiliar sensation of pure contentment and the sudden warmth which flooded through his veins until his heart felt as if it were on fire. Remember this moment, he told himself fiercely. Remember it for as long as you draw breath. He brushed aside the dark lock of hair which had fallen over her cheek and, lowering his head, he began to kiss her.

EPILOGUE

IT WASN'T, as Zahid remarked to Francesca on their wedding night, the most straightforward of unions. For the sheikh and his English bride began their married life with more challenges than most newly-wed couples had to contend with. But they had always known it would be that way.

First, there was the challenge of getting his country to accept a western wife who was also a commoner, rather than someone of noble blood who had been born and reared there. But here Frankie was at a definite advantage. Her late father had been known and adored by the people of Khayarzah—and her own obvious love of the culture shone through in all she did and said.

She charmed them by adopting a traditional Khayarzahian wedding gown for the emotional ceremony which took place over four days. And then proceeded to amaze them by saying her vows in flawless Khayarzahian—the product of her hard and ongoing work on the tricky language, for she was determined to be fluent one day. But mostly she was accepted because the people saw how deeply their king loved her. As she loved him. It was as clear as the night-time moon, they said.

So they named her Queen Anwar, which meant 'rays of light'. And the single wedding day photo which was issued to the world's media showed the two of them gazing rapt into each other's eyes, as if nothing outside that moment existed for either of them.

The second challenge was getting such a traditional male-led society to accept that changes were needed and that they *were* going to be made. The move to allowing women to drive and to attend universities didn't happen overnight, but it *did* happen, albeit very slowly. It came too late for Fayruz to go to college in her own country—but Frankie felt a fierce determination that the bright young girl should fulfil her intellectual potential. Thus, with her husband's blessing, the new queen sponsored her former servant to attend Cambridge University, where she excelled in both her degree subject of Middle Eastern politics, and on her college swimming team.

The final challenge was Frankie's alone. It meant saying goodbye to a way of life she had always known in England—and embracing a brand-new one in a desert land which was radically different. But that was no hardship for her, not even for a single second. Her father had taught her how to love Khayarzah, and she had loved Zahid from the very first moment she had known him. She would have walked to the ends of the earth for him.

In fact, she would do anything to make her beloved husband happy—and when he confided that he was worried about Tariq and the life he was leading, Frankie suggested inviting his brother to Khayarzah for an extended stay. Whether or not that would happen, who could say? Because Frankie knew that the future was like a handful of pebbles dropped to the ground—you never knew where they were going to fall.

Her only disappointment was in never seeing one of the fabled leopards, which her father had told her so much about—although she lived in hope. And Zahid regularly took her for a picnic in the lush foothills of the eastern heights, just in case. The place where they'd had their furious row—where their future had seemed so bleak and hopeless—had become their own, special place.

It was there that she told him that she was pregnant. And where one day—a month before she gave birth to their beautiful black-haired twins—he withdrew a slim leather box and handed it to her.

'What's this?' she questioned, with a smile.

'Why not open it and see?'

The chain was fine and gold and from it hung a glittering, stream-lined charm. A sleek animal, captured in mid-leap, its elegant body studded with diamonds and onyx—its eyes two rare and gleaming emeralds.

'Why, it's a leopard,' she said slowly as she held it up to the light and looked up at him with shining eyes.

Zahid's smile was tender as he took it from her and put it around her neck, fastening the clasp and then touching his lips to her neck in a lingering kiss. He moved round to pull her into his arms as the fertile swell of her belly pressed against him.

'Indeed it is. It's a way of saying that if reality doesn't always give you what you want, sweet Francesca—then you must reach out and create your own. Just as we have done.'

It was also, he knew, yet another way of telling her how much he loved her.

* * * * *

Mills & Boon® Large Print

January 2012

THE KANELLIS SCANDAL
Michelle Reid

MONARCH OF THE SANDS
Sharon Kendrick

ONE NIGHT IN THE ORIENT
Robyn Donald

HIS POOR LITTLE RICH GIRL
Melanie Milburne

FROM DAREDEVIL TO DEVOTED DADDY
Barbara McMahon

LITTLE COWGIRL NEEDS A MUM
Patricia Thayer

TO WED A RANCHER
Myrna Mackenzie

THE SECRET PRINCESS
Jessica Hart

Mills & Boon® Large Print
February 2012

THE MOST COVETED PRIZE
Penny Jordan

THE COSTARELLA CONQUEST
Emma Darcy

THE NIGHT THAT
CHANGED EVERYTHING
Anne McAllister

CRAVING THE FORBIDDEN
India Grey

HER ITALIAN SOLDIER
Rebecca Winters

THE LONESOME RANCHER
Patricia Thayer

NIKKI AND THE LONE WOLF
Marion Lennox

MARDIE AND THE CITY SURGEON
Marion Lennox

0112 Rom LP

Mills & Boon® Online

Discover more romance at
www.millsandboon.co.uk

- **FREE** online reads
- **Books** up to one month before shops
- **Browse our books** before you buy

...and much more!

For exclusive competitions and instant updates:

 Like us on **facebook.com/romancehq**

 Follow us on **twitter.com/millsandboonuk**

 Join us on **community.millsandboon.co.uk**

Visit us Online   Sign up for our FREE eNewsletter at
www.millsandboon.co.uk

WEB/M&B/RTL4/LP